Mahalo Memories

Boyd C. Hipp. II

Mahalo Books—Greer, SC
ISBN: 978-0-578-75763-6
Library of Congress Control Number: 2020918590
Title: Mahalo Memories
Author: Boyd C. Hipp. II
Digital distribution | 2020
Paperback | 2020

Dedication

To two remarkable men, my father Calhoun who finally got his wish to own a pleasure fishing yacht and to Hank, his captain, confidant and friend. From whom a unique relationship was forged, memories created and life lessons learned.

And to my children; Reeve, Elizabeth, Calhoun, Catherine and Thomas who inspire me every day.

And especially to my Lord and Savior, Jesus Christ. “Through Him all things are possible.” This book stands as proof of that!

A special thank you to Erica (Em) Hughes, publisher extraordinaire who guided me through this entire process making it as seamless as humanly possible.

Tight lines and good fishing!

Forward

Mahalo…according to the Hawaiian Dictionary means to thank or thanks, gratitude, compliment.

Between 1964-1976 a host of individuals had the unique opportunity to fish off the Hatteras Sport Fishing Yacht known as the Mahalo. This is a compilation of actual events placed in a fictional setting (I call it factional). For that reason, people, places and things may be moved, altered or otherwise changed to fit my tale. My thanks to all of you who shared your stories.

Chapter 1

Fall 1965

The early fall South Florida sun beat down at a temperature which reminded him of upstate South Carolina in mid-August. In other words, relentless.

The temperature did nothing to diminish the huge grin etched across his face. He finally had his dream toy, a 41' brand new Hatteras Sport Fisher, just delivered from the boatyard.

Now it gently rocked at its berth, slip F-142 at Pier 66 in Ft. Lauderdale. He had considered keeping the boat in Charleston, South Carolina but the run to the Gulfstream from there was further, which took longer and so why not really get away every time he went fishing. So, Ft. Lauderdale it was.

Calhoun had always been an analytical man. He had made his money overseeing investments for a mid-level insurance company and he took the same discipline when researching the boat he wanted. He had studied the boating industry ad nauseum and had concluded a Hatteras was the best boat for the buck given what he wanted to use it for. He had also taken that same approach in looking for a captain. He had researched the market, weighed the recommendations and decided on a young skipper, Captain Hank who was known for his boat handling skills as well as his ability to put his anglers “on the fish.” Hank was hired over the telephone, sight unseen.

Calhoun stood in the cockpit, flanked by dual fighting chairs and while he waited, he took a peek over the stern. MAHALO written in a bamboo stencil, ran the length of the back of the boat. His toy’s name, meaning “Thank You” in Hawaiian.

This moment, he thought, would be just perfect except for one thing…where in the hell was his captain?

Chapter 2

"Shit, shit, shit," screamed Hank, at no one in particular but at everyone within earshot. He was late to meet his new boss and was frustrated by the fact that a flat tire met him this morning as he was leaving home to prep the boat in anticipation of his boss's arrival only to be further delayed by the 17th Street Causeway Bridge stuck open which seemed to happen with great regularity but did it have to happen today?

He screeched into a parking space near the dock and sprinted across the mini golf course which separated the parking area from the boat slips. He ran up to the side and saw Calhoun, who was apparently napping in one of the fighting chairs which was an effect the Florida sun had on almost everybody. He knocked on the side of the boat. "Permission to come aboard."

To Hank's surprise, Calhoun was far from asleep as he slowly turned his head, sized up his new hire and responded with "If I waited much longer it would be lunch time. Pleased to meet you, please do come on board and let's see what we have here." Calhoun extended his hand in greeting, Hank took it and hopped onboard.

Hank had "learned" his new boat during the time he brought it down from Hatteras to Lauderdale. So, for the next hour, Hank showed Calhoun where everything was located and gave him a cursory overview of how everything worked. From the flying bridge to the main salon to the staterooms to the engine room, Hank went over it all.

"Mr. Hipp, I want at least one other person to know how to run this boat in case it becomes necessary. Now let me show you the engine room. You are able to access it from behind the stairs leading from the main salon to the sleeping quarters."

Hank removed the stairs thus revealing a doorway that led to the engines. He duck-walked into the engine compartment followed by Calhoun. "Normally, if we had been running today, the temperature in this area would be too hot to access. Do you see anything that looks unusual?"

Calhoun looked around the compact area, not really sure what he should be looking for. "I don't think so."

"Look over to that outside wall. What do you see?"

Calhoun looked for a moment and nonchalantly replied, "I can see the water line through the fiberglass."

"Exactly! I have spent my entire career on wood boats and this new concept of fiberglass is nothing but unnerving. I don't think you should be able to tell where the outside water is."

"Well, Hank, I have studied the science on this, which is why I decided on one of the first fiberglass production boats. It is sturdier and easier to maintain. Now get me out of here…it is way too cramped for me!" remarked Calhoun, "Let's see how she handles on the water."

"That suits me."

For it was on the water where Hank was really in his element and he was excited to have an owner who wanted to use their boat for the purpose it was designed…deep sea fishing.

Chapter 3

Spring 1966
Bimini, Bahamas

Calhoun sprawled on one of the two fighting chairs, allowing the fading rays of the warm Bahamian sun to work its magic by lulling him into a dream state. This was the first trip with Hank to this fishing paradise and so far, it had been a successful one with multiple dolphin (known as Mahi Mahi) caught in addition to a couple of sails raised but not boated…and it was just the first day!

Hank was down below, prepping the dolphin for dinner by marinating them in freshly squeezed limes. The Mahalo rocked gently at its berth at the Bimini Big Game Fishing Club which would be their island home for the next few days. Calhoun slowly nursed his scotch and water while enjoying his ever-present pipe. Down below, Hank was also relaxing with his signature drink of Bacardi Rum and Coke with a lime.

If this wasn't as close to heaven as one could get, he didn't know what was, mused Calhoun.

Hank popped his head out from the main salon "Mind if I join you?"

"Come ahead, I could use the company."

Hank settled into the other fighting chair. "We had a pretty good day today but I think tomorrow will be better if you are up for shoving off around six a.m."

“Suits me. I didn’t fly all the way from Greenville to sleep in. I want to put this baby to use!”

“Perfect.” Hank was grinning ear to ear over the prospect of a great day on the water. “Tell me Mr. Hipp, if you don’t mind me asking, how did you decide on deep sea fishing as a hobby coming from a land locked city like Greenville, South Carolina?”

“Well, as you know, I had to wait for my divorce to be final before I could purchase this gem so it would not be considered an asset. Once that was done, I had to choose between Charleston, which is right on our coast, or some other eastern seaboard port. I considered Charleston but the Gulf Stream was a long run while it is only about thirty minutes from Ft. Lauderdale and, well, Ft. Lauderdale? Seems to me an obvious choice. And we are only a three-hour run to Bimini!”

Hank nodded his head in silent affirmation of his boss’s choice. “Well, let me get this dinner up…Captain Hanks world famous dolphin with a mixed salad and peas and rice on the way!”

Chapter 4

The meal exceeded every expectation and after they cleaned up Calhoun suggested they take a stroll into Alice Town to help settle their food.

Passing by the entrance to the Big Game Club, Hank and Calhoun took a left onto the main street of Alice Town. The hard-packed sand road was ideal for pedestrians as there were few vehicles on the island other than police and small delivery trucks. They passed the small bungalow which housed the Bimini Bakery, some of the best bread Calhoun had ever tasted, which Hank had introduced to him earlier that evening over dinner. Continuing down the road Calhoun was assaulted by the aromas coming from The Red Lion.

"Hank, whatever they are cooking smells delicious."

"It is every bit as good as it smells Mr. Hipp. We will try it out tomorrow and if we are lucky, they will prepare anything we catch."

"Now that sounds like a plan."

Continuing down the street, they ended up at the Compleat Angler, home to Hemingway's Bar, which had hosted the author numerous times when he fished off of Bimini.

"Let me suggest a nightcap and let you look at some of the memorabilia scattered throughout this place" suggested Hank. "It is supposed to house the largest collection of Hemingway artifacts outside of Key West."

They stepped onto the docks and before they could get to the entry to the bar, they heard the screaming of a hotly disputed argument or assault. It was difficult to tell which it may be.

The bar door flung over and the two of them were nearly knocked over by a young woman fleeing the bar.

"LEAVE ME ALONE, SLAYDER!" she screamed. "I want no part of any of this." And with that she disappeared at a dead sprint down the main road, heading back toward the area Hank and Calhoun had just come from.

"BITCH! You have nowhere to go on this island. I'll find you and when I do you will be sorry."

The pursuer pulled up just short of where Calhoun and Hank stood and seemed to realize for the first time that they were there.

"What do you two want?" he snarled.

"A drink" both men said in unison which would have been comical if the air wasn't so charged with open hostility.

"Outta my way old man." Before he could shove past, he leaned back into the door and yelled, "Tom, Jerry, let's go! We need to find that bitch so I can teach her a lesson!"

Hank and Calhoun stood aside allowing the three to pass. After they had gone, Calhoun bent over and grabbed his knees, doubled up in laughter. "Tom? Jerry? Really? Is this a cartoon gang? Let's go have that drink!"

"Fine by me," as Hank started toward the door. He looked back down the dock where the three thugs had just gone, for he could not think of them as anything but thugs, picking on some young girl. Yet, he couldn't shake the feeling that this was not the last he would be seeing of them.

Chapter 5

Calhoun was awakened the next morning by the twin engines cranking up. He looked at his watch and saw it was just a bit before six a.m. Well, Hank had said it would be an early and productive day. He lay in the bed for another moment when he suddenly realized he was hearing voices…who was it? Had those punks somehow found the Mahalo and were harassing Hank?

Jumping out of bed, he raced up the stairs in his boxers, through the main saloon and slid the door open to the cockpit only to be greeted by a huge native.

"Good Morning Sir" welcomed the stranger. "My name is Bones and I will be your first mate."

"Ahh, I see you met Bones" observed Hank as he came down the dock with bagged ice for the bait and fish boxes along with fresh bait for the days fishing. "I've known Bones since he was a child and I've trained him to be the finest first mate between North and South Bimini if I do say so myself." He tossed the bagged ice to Bones and jumped on board. "Ready to catch dinner?"

Calhoun realized he was still in his boxers after running up to the cockpit having feared the company they may have was not nearly as affable as the company they actually had.

"Let me change into my fishing shorts and I'll be ready."

"Great. Bones, I'll get the spring and stern lines if you'll get up to the flying bridge and take us out. Bow line will be last line I grab."

As they headed for the jetties leading out of the two islands, Hank busied himself in rigging up the baits for the days fishing. Calhoun took advantage of the opportunity to inquire further about Bones.

"Tell me about our first mate, Captain."

"Well, he is the product of a long-standing relationship between a friend of mine, another captain, and a local. He gets his name from his adoptive father, Bonefish Rudy, who is one of the best local guides for bone fishing these flats. He started working on the docks as many of the locals do by washing down boats as they came in from a day of fishing. He was only six when he caught my eye. He was scared to death when he came up to me to ask if he could help wash the boat down. But he got over his nervousness real quick as he learned that properly washing down a boat is not an easy task. But he stayed with it and by the time he was eight I had him rigging baits which he could do as well as anyone. By then he was bugging me to take him out fishing as my first mate but he was way too young so he just hung around the docks, listening to all the fish stories from that day of fishing like who caught what, where. That way he learned where all the fishing holes were. I gave him a couple of books to read and taught him how to clean fish. From those two sources he got all the education he needed. He was ready to put into practice what he thought he knew. So, I promised I would take him out with me to celebrate his birthday when he turned ten. He has been with me ever since…going on twelve years or so now."

As Hank spoke, he was also busy rigging the fishing rods for the upcoming day of fishing. He had just unspooled the leader wire on the number three pole when Bones yelled down "Captain get a bait in the water, double quick!"

Hank knew better than to question his mate but they were still in the harbor, not yet clearing the jetties to the ocean. It was just then that Bones took the boat out of gear and allowed the momentum to keep her moving forward. Hank loosened the drag as the bait of Ballyhoo played out behind the Mahalo.

"JIG" Screamed Bones. "Jig, jig, jig!" which immediately sent Hank into a whipsawing motion with the rod making the bait seem alive.

Then he saw what Bones had spotted earlier…a sail! A damn sail in the harbor! Not totally unheard of but highly unusual. "Sit down Mr. Hipp! Grab that chair next to me!" Hank continued to jig hoping to entice the fish to take the bait. No sooner had Calhoun maneuvered around Hank and plopped into the chair than he witnessed a sight he would see many times. The sail leapt into the air and crashed the bait. Then the intricate dance of hunter and prey began.

Hank handed the rod to Calhoun who placed it in the gimbal between his legs and started to reel, smooth cranking as he would lower the rod then pull the pole back toward him and reel going down, repeating the motion as he attempted to bring the fish closer to the boat.

"Well, it looks like we may have an audience" observed the captain. And indeed a few folks had gathered on the docks, no doubt preparing for their own day of fishing but frozen in place as they bore witness to this rare occurrence of a sailfish being caught inside the harbor. Then Calhoun saw her, the girl from last night, standing alone on one of the piers grinning while silently applauding the scene playing out before her.

Calhoun grinned back, not even sure if she could tell from the distance between them that he was smiling, when he heard a huge POP! The line had broken, the fish was gone and his ego along with it.

"One thing boss you need to remember. Keep the line tight. You allow slack in the line and you can almost guarantee it will break. You need to focus on the task at hand" Calhoun felt chastised enough until he heard Bones swear "DAMN."

He looked back toward the source of his distraction, the pretty blonde from the previous evening. She was nowhere to be seen.

Chapter 6

They rounded the corner of North Bimini and made for open water. Both Hank and Calhoun took the opportunity to climb up to the flying bridge before Bones opened up the throttles to head toward deeper water. The mood wasn't exactly glum but both Hank and Bones realized they had lost a unique opportunity in not being able to boat a billfish caught in the harbor. But there were always other fish. Hank reached into one of the lockers and pulled out a pair of binoculars. Standing to the side of the bridge, he braced against the captain's chair in order to give himself a sturdier platform to scan the ocean in front of him. The sun was gaining purchase in the sky behind them so at least he did not have to contend with those blinding rays. He seemed to freeze for a moment, staring at one spot off on the horizon. "Bones, take us over in this direction" pointing to an area off the starboard bow. "I believe I see birds working in that direction."

Calhoun was somewhat confused by the terminology which must have shown on his face because Hank continued on. "By working, I mean they are circling and diving over a particular area which usually means there are bait fish there and where there are bait fish, there are usually larger fish feeding on them."

Calhoun nodded, simply stating, "Makes sense."

It took about twenty minutes to get close enough to the birds to see what was attracting them. On the surface, stretching for several hundred yards was a line of seaweed, which is where dolphin liked to gather. But there was something else in the middle of the seaweed which really caught Hank's attention.

"Bones, throttle back and give me some time to change into a bathing suit. In the meantime, aim for that object floating at about two o'clock." Before Bones could respond Hank had grabbed the handrails on the ladder leading below sliding down without even bothering to use the steps. No more than five minutes later he was back in his swimsuit carrying a hand spear, dive mask with snorkel and flippers along with a mesh bag.

"OK Bones bring us up to that object but keep about twenty yards off." As Bones brought the Mahalo adjacent to the object, he suddenly realized what it was…a fifty-five gallon drum, floating just below the surface. This is a marine hazard if I ever saw one, he thought. Perhaps Hank is going to try and sink it before someone runs over it and really screws up their boat.

No sooner than the thought had crossed his mind than he heard the slight splash indicating Hank was in the water. Bones looked over from the flying bridge and could see Hank on the surface with mask and fins on, effortlessly snorkeling toward the drum. Suddenly, he disappeared below the surface. A moment later he returned for air and dove again, going under the drum. This process was repeated a handful of additional times before he started swimming back to the Mahalo, holding the mesh dive bag above his head as if it were some kind of fragile trophy.

Calhoun stood in the cockpit, ready to grab whatever Hank had in the bag. With the engines off, the Mahalo drifted alongside the weed line, the gentle swells causing the boat to slightly rock back and forth. While Hank made his way back, Calhoun had a moment to pause to take in the crystal clear, emerald green water. The blue skies above gave a picturesque contrast to the ocean…pastel colors in abundance. He was glad they had gotten an early start especially since he could see a number of boats disgorging from the mouth of the harbor, all headed out for a day of fishing.

Calhoun was so lost in his daydream Hank's surfacing next to where he stood actually startled him.

"Whatcha got there captain?"

"Fresh lobster tails" came the response as he tossed the mesh dive bag to Calhoun and hauled himself up on the three-foot dive platform attached to the stern of the boat.

Hank swung his legs over the transom and stepped into the cockpit. Bones was up top, standing at the rail overlooking the fishing area waiting for some explanation

"So, when I saw the birds working, I figured we had us a couple of schools of dolphin. What I did not reckon on until we got closer and I could put the glasses on her was that drum. It's apparently someone's makeshift lobster trap as the underbelly is cut out and baited with fish heads. Must be 30 or 40 lobsters in there. I took a dozen, twisted their tails off and stuffed them in my bag. We got dinner tonight guys! Bones, fire up the engines and let's make a couple of loops around this weed line to see if we can catch anything before the rest of those boats figure out what we are up to. I'm going below for a quick shower."

"WAIT! How did you deal with their claws?" inquired Calhoun.

"No problem. Unlike their Yankee cousins, Bahamian lobsters have no claws to speak of so it makes grabbing them easy as long as you can catch them."

And with that, Hank vanished into the main salon and headed below. In the meantime, Bones put the throttles forward at a dead slow and headed on a course perpendicular to the weed line so when he put the lines out the bait would not get fouled with seaweed. All Calhoun could do was observe, which suited him fine as it gave him a chance to pull out his pipe and light up a bowl of Prince Albert.

After all the lines were out and in their respective outriggers, Bones started trolling a course which paralleled the weed line staying about fifteen yards off of it. By the time Hank finished his shower, the only action had been the Ballyhoo getting fouled by the seaweed and the extra weight on the baits causing them to get knocked out of the clips holding them to the outriggers.

"Nothing so far captain."

"Let's continue to run up the weed line on this side and come back down on the other. Surely something is hanging around here unless I spooked them when I checked out the lobster barrel."

Bones did as instructed but to no avail as the ocean suddenly seemed totally void of fish. The sun was climbing higher in the cloudless sky and as it climbed, so did the temperature.

"Hank, where are the fish?" chided Calhoun from the cockpit below. "It's hot down here and…."

"THREE, THREE, THREE, GRAB IT MR. HIPP" came the scream from Hank as he slid down the ladder to the deck below. "SIT DOWN QUICK" Hank barked the order as he grabbed the rod sitting in the three hole and started to jig. He kept the motion up while releasing the drag allowing the bait to fall back. He continued to jig furiously when suddenly the ZING of the line spilling off the reel indicated a hooked fish.

"Got it! Alright Mr. Hipp, here you go," as he placed the rod in the holder between the legs of his boss. Calhoun grabbed the rod, which was bent over seemingly 45 degrees as the line continued to scream off the reel.

"Keep the rod up and reel!"

"Reel my ass, it's all I can do to hang on! Did you see what it is?"

"Don't you worry about that. You just keep that line tight. I don't want a repeat of this morning. The fish will no doubt make a run toward the boat. Reel fast when he does and can keep the line tight. I'm going up topside and will send Bones down in a minute. Oh, and did I say keep the line tight?"

Before Calhoun could object, Hank had already taken the ladder up two steps at a time.

"Did you see it Cap? I was busy looking forward keeping us out of the weed line."

"Looked to be a marlin and a damn big one at that. Better get down there with the boss. This could be a long fight." Hank glanced at his watch as he spoke. It was dead on 11:30.

The first thing Bones did, upon reaching the cockpit, was to reel in the other three lines thus clearing the decks for the fight at hand. Even though it was early into the battle, he went below into the engine compartment where the largest gaff was stored and brought it up to the cockpit.

"Good God!" exclaimed Calhoun. "We gonna need that huge hook?"

"Looks like it," smiled Bones.

Hank looked over the rail from the flying bridge, "You girls finished with your tea party? I hope so cause we have a fish to catch but don't let that interrupt you!"

Bones and Calhoun took the hint although it was difficult to focus on anything else. Calhoun could really do nothing more than watch the line spool out as the marlin ran deep.

Just as quickly as the line played out it suddenly stopped. "Reel fast Mr. Hipp. She's coming to the surface and we need that line tight," ordered Hank.

For a good two minutes Calhoun reeled in the line as fast as he could. In fact, his arm was beginning to cramp when, without warning, the marlin shot straight up into the air and began to tail dance on the surface. What stunned Calhoun was the size of the fish. It seemed to blot out the sky behind it. "So, this is what Hemingway experienced" was his immediate thought as the fish fell back on his side into the water.

"REEL!" barked Hank.

Calhoun was rewarded for his efforts with another breach of the surface by his competitor but this time only the head came above the surface, wagging furiously in a futile attempt to throw the hook. He was also spewing blood.

"Shit!" screamed Hank. "I'm going to back down on this fish real quick so keep reeling. Bones, this fish is still green so be careful with that gaff."

With that, Hank threw the engines into reverse and started toward the fish with Calhoun bringing the line in as fast as he could to avoid getting it tangled in the propellers. Bones was stationed just behind Calhoun, turning his seat as necessary in order to keep a straight line between angler and fish.

Without warning, a series of heavy tugs hit the line, providing tension where a moment ago there was none.

"Damn it to hell" yelled Hank. He continued to back toward the fish but even Calhoun could tell something was wrong. When the leader wire got to the boat, Bones leaned over the transom, gaff in hand and hooked the fish. With a grunt he leaned back and brought in only the head from the gills up. The rest of the fish was gone.

"What the…?" But before Calhoun could finish his question Hank was already talking.

"Sharks. I was afraid of that when I saw how much blood he was losing. He had to have been gut hooked…swallowed the hook and it tore up his insides. After that it was only a matter of time before the sharks got here."

"Well what good is the head?" quizzed Calhoun.

"We'll take it back to the dock and weigh it. From there we can reasonably guess what the total weight might have been. That's only good for future fish stories about the one that got away. Boys, we are 0 for 2 today. It's 2 o'clock…how about lunch?

Calhoun did not feel hungry until he realized he had fought that denizen of the deep for 2 ½ hours. Then he was famished!

There are no such things as "lunch breaks" when Hank is in command. The three men took turns going below and making a quick sandwich which was consumed near their "action stations," usually eaten while standing. In the meantime, Hank was steering a race course pattern, basically a large figure 8 using the weed line as its mid-point. After two hours of this trolling, Hank called down to Bones and Calhoun.

"Let's bring in the lines and head back. At least we have some lobster we can get grilled at the Red Lion tonight. And Bones, once we wash down the boat, why don't you join us for dinner so we can discuss where we are going to fish tomorrow."

"Ok by me Cap. You don't have to ask me twice for a lobster dinner!" Even though the prospect of dinner was enticing, all three men were left to ponder what might have been from the days fishing.

Chapter 7

It took about forty-five minutes to get back to the dock and to tie up at the Big Game Club. By the time Hank had hooked up to shore power and gotten two hoses ready to wash down the boat, Bones had returned with a wheelbarrow to take the marlin head to the weigh station so they could get an estimate of what the entire fish may have weighed. "Cap, I will be right back. Gonna figure out what this guy weighed."

"Or, give me a reason to avoid washing down the boat" retorted Hank. "Don't worry, there'll be plenty left for you to do when you return. And Bones, grab those lobster tails and take them on to the Red Lion and let them know we will be up in a while."

"Will do."

Washing down a fishing boat after a day on the sea sounds simplistic on its surface but is more complex and tedious than you might expect. It has to be, due to the corrosive nature of salt water and salt air. First comes the rinsing of the entire boat, followed by soaping it up, then rinsing again and finished off with drying the entire outside surface with a chamois. Once all of that is done, canvas covers are placed over the control panels, windshield and captain's chair on the flying bridge as well as the fighting chairs in the cockpit. The complete process, if done correctly, can take 90 minutes with the timeframe being reduced by the number of folks working on the cleanup. This does not include rinsing and drying the rods and reels and returning them to their holders inside the main salon or the cleaning of any fish which may have been caught that day.

Calhoun began in the stern washing down the rods and reels, drying them and putting them away. Hank was on the bow of the boat rinsing it down when Bones returned with a small army trailing behind him.

"Seems we may be stars for a day, Hank. Word has gotten around about the sail we hooked inside the harbor and when I took the head up to weigh, folks started to gather. By the way, Mr. Hipp, that marlin would have come in around 700-750 pounds according to the dockmaster. Also, Mr. Holmes at the Big Game Club wants to speak with you about their keeping the head and having it mounted and hung in the club. Even though we did not get the entire fish, it seems we have the potential largest marlin caught for the season. It won't be official of course."

"To hell with protocol" declared Hank. "If it's ok with you Mr. Hipp, I'm going to run up the marlin flag signifying we boated one. Even if it was just a head."

"That's ok with me. At 700 pounds no wonder the damn fish blocked the sky! Bones, what's with all the people tagging along behind you?"

"They wanted to come see the guy who caught that harbor sail."

"HEY! Remember me? I don't know about you two but I'm hungry and its way past my rum and coke time so if you two could get busy cleaning the boat the sooner we can get to cocktail hour" instructed Hank.

Chapter 8

With three of them working, the cleanup took less than an hour. Due to the hour and their plans to get an early start in the morning, they decided to have their drinks at the restaurant. As they made their way down the dock into Alice Town, Calhoun could not help but notice several boats were flying either sailfish or marlin flags from their outriggers denoting the fact they had caught one during the days fishing. Those flags would fly until the boat went back out to fish. "Son of a bitch!" thought Calhoun. "We should have had at least one of those if not two."

The Red Lion was less than a five-minute walk and the proprietor was standing at the door chatting with one of the locals when they arrived.

"Good to see you Hank. Heard you had a most interesting day. I have grilled the lobster tails for you and thought some Wahoo steaks would go nicely."

"Thanks, Woody. That sounds good. By the way, meet my boss, Calhoun Hipp. He is from the upstate of South Carolina not far from you."

"Really? I'm from Spartanburg. Proud expatriate of the area. Came down here once I graduated Wofford College and have not looked back. Welcome to my humble establishment."

"Thanks. Always good to meet a fellow traveler from the Palmetto State," replied Calhoun.

The three men grabbed a table as Woody disappeared into the kitchen to oversee the meal prep for his guests. After a round of drinks, Hank laid out the plans for the next day. They decided to shove off around 5:30 the next morning so they could be on station at a place Hank liked just north of the island. No one wanted to be skunked again.

The meal came without further fanfare and proved to be thoroughly enjoyable with the pairing of lobster and Wahoo accompanied by grilled vegetables, warm Bimini bread and topped off with a key lime pie prepared island style.

After they said their goodbyes to Woody, Calhoun suggested they head back up the street so he could enjoy his pipe before they all turned in. The evening was a perfect temperature with no humidity and a hint of a breeze. A night that just made you glad to be alive. In other words, full of contentment between the weather and the meal.

Finally, Hank suggested they head back toward the boat and turn in as they had a long day ahead of them. Hearing no objections, they returned in silence as each of them were lost in their own thoughts.

When they got back to the docks, Hank asked Bones to go buy some additional baits and ice since he knew the tackle shop would not yet be open at the time they had planned to leave. Calhoun and Hank had barely stepped onto the boat when they heard a huge ruckus; the sound of pounding feet on the dock coming their way. Calhoun had just turned around to see what was going on when the pretty blonde from last night sprinted up to the boat.

"Please help me. Those guys from last night are after me" she gasped bent over, hands on her knees as she tried to get her wind.

Without thinking Calhoun extended his hand. "Come aboard and tell us what is going on."

Those words were barely out of his mouth before the three guys from last evening rounded the corner and saw the girl standing on the Mahalo.

"Eva, you bitch. I don't know what you think you are doing but get your ass back up here."

"Hold on young man" replied Calhoun. "What's this all about?"

"None of your business old man."

"Well, since she is on my boat, it's my business now."

The three started to move toward the boat just as Hank appeared in the salon doorway. "Stop right there! You have no right, nor permission to board this boat."

"Two old men, big whoop! Just give us back the girl."

"Better make that three against three…seems to be better odds." The thugs turned to see Bones standing behind them. "I'd get out of here if I was you while you still can."

Tom and Jerry both looked over to Slayder for guidance. They could tell from the look on his face he was seriously weighing whether to try and grab the girl.

"NOW!" Hank yelled so loud it caused all three thugs to jump. The tension seemed to melt at that moment. Slayder looked back at Eva and with a withering stare growled "I'll be back."

"Not tonight kid or ever if you know what's good for you." said Bones, matching stare for stare.

With the immediate threat diminished, the three men looked at one another silently conveying a 'now what do we do?' question between them.

Calhoun was the first to break the silence. "Ok young lady, why don't we start with what this is all about and who you are?"

Bones, Hank and Calhoun soon learned her name was Eva Knox, from Thompson, Georgia who thought she was heading to Bimini for a getaway weekend only to discover her new boyfriend was involved in smuggling drugs into the U.S. This explained the other two guys he had met up with over here, neither of which she had ever seen before.

She pleaded with Calhoun to let her stay the night promising she would be gone before they headed out to fish in the morning.

"I'm not sure if staying here solves your problem" observed Calhoun. "Bimini is a small island, nowhere you can really hangout until you can catch one of Chalks seaplanes out of here. Not to mention those guys seem pretty relentless and determined to get you back. I think the best thing we can do is for us to get you back stateside. Can you get your passport?"

"Yes, it's in the hotel safe at the Compleat Angler."

"I can get that no problem" volunteered Bones. "My cousin Bowers is the night clerk there and he'll give it to me no questions. Since it does not seem like we are fishing tomorrow, I'll stand watch tonight when I get back in case those jerks try something stupid. I'll be back in a bit."

Hank took the lead "Eva come with me, I'll show you where the guest quarters are and get you squared away. Mr. Hipp?"

"Think I'll sit out here for a minute and have a smoke. Damn strange day, all the way around."

Chapter 9

Which awoke him first, the engines starting or the smell of coffee brewing? It didn't matter as Calhoun shook the cobwebs from his head, threw his legs over the side of the bed and groggily headed out to the main salon. He was shocked to see Eva already there, sitting on the couch, cup in hand with her legs tucked beneath her.

"Good Morning Mr. Hipp."

"Eva, it's Calhoun. I trust you slept ok?"

"As well as I could. I cannot thank you enough for letting me stay on board last night. I feel like I have been enough trouble so I may just try to avoid Slayder and his friends and catch Chalks out of here later today."

"First of all, it has been no trouble. Secondly, you trying to hide until Chalks arrives is foolish and thirdly, Chalks being a seaplane, it may or may not be able to land here in the harbor, just depends on the chop. I thought we settled this last night. Besides, it's three hours back to Lauderdale and I could use the company. You owe me that much."

Seeing there was no way out, Eva nodded her consent as Hank came into the salon. "Obviously, Bones had no trouble last night from your friends. He did find out from his cousin Bowers when he went to fetch your passport that those Tom and Jerry characters are real trouble. Have been using South

Bimini as their base of operations, flying drugs into the airstrip over there since it is an uncontrolled field. Word is the officials over there may have their hand out to look the other way."

"Well, that's behind us now. Hank, I was thinking maybe we could troll for a bit as we head back home, maybe even catch something worth keeping since we already have the bait on board and I noticed Bones had already rigged the lines for fishing."

"Yeah, he was bored last night so he made himself useful. I like your fishing idea boss, so let's go!"

Chapter 10

They cleared the jetties within fifteen minutes. Unlike the day before, there was no fish on the line, no audience watching. Hank ran the boat full tilt for an additional forty-five minutes until Bimini was little more than a smudge on the horizon. His reasoning was twofold. First, he wanted distance between himself and those druggies he had left behind. The second, was more important for it was here the ocean floor gave way from the area known as the Bimini Shelf falling away to the deeper gulf stream, rich in schools of fish; hunters and hunted. Given the early start, they were the only ones out. Hank reeled out the lines and placed two in the outriggers with the other two in the rod holders on the fighting chairs. Eva took her seat along rods three and four. The seas were running a mild two to three feet causing a gentle swell but giving the ocean enough action as to attract fish to the surface. Hank had scampered back up to the flying bridge and was settling in with his second cup of coffee.

"ZIP ZING" came the scream of the line popping out of the outrigger.

"FOUR, FOUR" yelled Hank. "That's yours Eva in the holder on the side!"

Eva leaned over and tried to get the rod out but found she could not get it out due to the weight of the fish she had on her line.

"I, I can't get it out of the holder and into the cup," she whimpered.

"First of all, baseball players have cups! That holder between your legs is a gimbal. Now stop your whining and get busy fishing!" admonished Hank as he descended from the bridge to give her a hand. "In the meantime, Mr. Hipp, please get those other lines in. We don't want anything fouling them."

As Calhoun busied himself with clearing the lines, he glanced over to Eva and watched. Her face was contorted partially from strain, partially from frustration and for the first time he really took note of how striking she was. He had not failed earlier to notice the long legs spilling out of her cut off jeans or the fact she wore a halter top with obviously no bra.

Eva began the routine of reeling in by lowering her rod, reeling hard and then bringing the rod back to her in order to maintain a constant pressure on the line. This fish was not going to get the opportunity to throw a hook. After fifteen minutes Hank put the boat in neutral and slid down the ladder to the cockpit. He put on gloves and grabbed a gaff. Yelling at Eva to reel hard, he leaned over the transom and made one stab then a second stab which impaled the fish perfectly.

With both hands he leaned back and swung the fish onboard, gasping from the weight of the fish. "Dolphin, and a big one too! Mr. Hipp, open the fish box and Eva when I get this fish in there, jump on and sit on the top cause this fish still has some fight and I don't want it flopping out."

Everyone did as instructed and the fish was secured in the fish box.

“I’d say that fish is about forty pounds or so. A good size which will make for an excellent dinner tonight. Since dinner was our goal, everyone ok with hightailing it back to Pier 66?”

Hearing nothing to the contrary, Hank quickly washed down the cockpit soiled from the blood off the fish and put the throttles full forward as they made for home.

Thirty minutes later, Hank heard his name being gently called. It was Eva. Pulling the throttles back, he looked over the rail down into the cockpit. “Yes ma’am”

“I feel really bad about that fish. Can we just put him back?”

Hank wasn’t sure he heard correctly. “Say again.”

“My fish. I want to put him back.”

“You do know he is not alive. He has been out of the water for over a half an hour and has a huge gash in his side from the gaff to boot.”

“I just looked at him. He’s still alive cause his eyes are still open.”

Hank looked at Calhoun for guidance only to have a shrug of his shoulders indicate he was as perplexed as the captain.

With a huge and intentionally loud sigh, Hank came down and pulled the fish from the box. Wiggling it back and forth to make it appear alive he gently placed the dolphin back into the ocean. Since they are relatively flat fish, she slowly sank.

“See! See! I told you it was alive! See, its swimming away! Thank you, Hank,” grabbing the captain and giving him a full body hug, which left him blushing. “WELL! I never!” Hank said in mock shock as he gently untangled himself from Eva and scampered back to the bridge.

As Hank throttled back up, Calhoun leaned over his chair, asking Eva to join him in the other fighting seat. He really had not appraised her before but did so now. She was beautiful, no better way to describe her. Her blonde locks were pulled into a ponytail underneath a baseball cap inscribed with just the word Bimini across the front. Her legs betrayed a 5’9” frame chiseled from what could only be a result of a constant workout regimen. But it was the eyes Calhoun thought to himself, wasn’t it always the eyes which provided the true window into the soul. Hers were the most beguiling shade of green he had ever seen, highlighted with what could only be described as flecks of gold scattered throughout her pupils. Almost other worldly, he thought and surely camouflaging certain wisdom beyond her time with just a hint of crow’s feet on the edges of her eyes disguising a great deal of mirth, as though only she knew the joke.

“Eva, tell me about you. How did you get mixed up with that bunch?”

What followed was a long dissertation. Calhoun learned she had grown up in Thompson, Georgia, had attended boarding school in Virginia as well as college, loved to show horses and had spent the last three years actually using her college major by teaching special education. She had met Slayder about three months ago at a party but had only been out on a couple of dates until he asked her to come to Bimini which she now realized provided him a cover story to hide his true intent of setting up a drug route into the states.

When she finished, Calhoun stood to stretch his legs and was startled they were almost back to Fort Lauderdale. “Where do you go from here?” he asked.

“I have a condo at Bahia Mar. In fact, I insist you let me cook dinner tonight to thank you for rescuing me. And especially since I made us release the dolphin you guys had planned on cooking for dinner.”

“That’s not necessary.”

“Maybe not, but it will make me feel better and it will give me a chance to learn a little more about you. It’s unit P-4. Be there at eight p.m. sharp.”

It was settled before it even became a discussion. Calhoun had the feeling this was not unusual when it came to dealing with this vixen!

Chapter 11

He rang the doorbell precisely at eight sharp. The chimes inside were answered by a sudden eruption of yapping. "A dog? She never said anything about a dog."

Before he could think further on it, the door swung open and there stood Eva in a shear, ankle length white cotton caftan which had become translucent due to the setting sun streaming in from the floor to ceiling windows set on the wall behind her. It left nothing to the imagination which was no surprise since there was nothing between her and the dress.

"Come in" she cooed after giving him a quick kiss on the lips. "Forgive me, I have something in the oven so make yourself at home" turning to walk back down the hallway. He no sooner had closed the door than he was savaged by a miniature white poodle running furiously around his legs.

"Don't worry, that's just Snickerdoodle."

Calhoun could not contain his laughter over the name. "Snickerdoodle?"

"Don't laugh Calhoun, he is very sensitive to his name."

In the meantime, the dog continued to run in ever decreasing circles almost causing Calhoun to trip over him in the entry foyer.

Suddenly, the dog keeled over.

"Oh my God," thought Calhoun. "The dog just died!"

"EVA!"

The urgency in his voice made Eva drop what she was doing in the kitchen and come running. Calhoun could only look at her with horror. She stopped when she saw her pet and calmly walked to Calhoun putting a comforting hand on his arm. "Don't worry, the dog has only fainted. He does that sometimes when he gets worked up. Believe me he does not get that way with just anyone so you should feel complimented. Leave him be, he'll be fine. Come on in."

Shaking his head in disbelief, he followed her in, leaving her pet to come around on his own. He was so lost in his thoughts he didn't realize Eva had stopped and abruptly turned around until he almost bumped into her.

"Look, Calhoun. People tell me I am a free spirit, full of imagination while being sensitive all at the same time. I don't know, maybe that is something you will find out over time. What I do know is I know what I want and I have been attracted to you since the moment I stepped on the Mahalo."

Before he could even muster a reply, she had closed the remaining gap between them and had fully pressed her lips and her body against his.

"I know I said I would fix dinner tonight" she whispered. "Maybe later" and with that she pulled on the straps of her dress, causing it to drop, where it pooled around her ankles.

"My God, she is gorgeous" he marveled as he stroked her silky skin amazed at how soft she felt. He cupped her face between his hands, allowing her blonde hair to fall across her shoulders as he pulled back the hair which swept over her left eye ala Veronica Lake. "I am the moth" he thought. "She is the flame and a white-hot flame at that." He was smitten and he knew it.

"Let's go" Eva said, grabbing his arm and leading him toward her bedroom. "I wanna butt snuggle."

"What's that?" he croaked, suddenly as nervous as a high schooler on his first time.

"I'll show you."

And so, she did.

Later, they sat on her deck, looking over the marina, enjoying the mild temperature and star filled South Florida evening. Snickerdoodle had found a new best friend and was snuggled up in Calhoun's lap.

"Well, now that we have taken that first, and I might add, enjoyable step, perhaps it's time I learn more about you. Who is Calhoun Hipp?"

"In a nutshell, I come from upstate South Carolina, a rather large family, went off to school and later to college in North Carolina. World War II was still going on when I graduated so I went into the Army, saw action at the Battle of the Bulge, got wounded, came home and helped my two older brothers manage a mid-sized insurance company by running their investment department. Worked hard until I decided it was time to enjoy the fruits of my labors. Resigned, and now here I am."

"Large family? How many?"

"Aside from Francis and Herman, there is Elizabeth, Sarah, Charlie, Caroline, Annie, Cate, LC,

Hodges along with Dot, Hayne, Gail and others I probably have not even met yet."

"WOW! You can tell this was before the age of television! I want to hear all about them."

"Somehow, I think we will have the time."

Chapter 12

Summer 1967

They were a couple, at least that's the way Eva viewed it, in a schoolgirl, first crush, giddy way as she sat in the cockpit of the Mahalo, headed back to Bimini for the first time since she had met Calhoun. They had been together for a year so it made sense to head back to the very place they had first met to celebrate their one-year dating anniversary. What a whirlwind it had been! Trips to Key Largo Florida and the Ocean Reef Club fishing their way to Key West and back. Running up the east coast to Charleston so he could show Eva the Holy City as he knew it and later to Bald Head Island where they felt time had slowed down. The year had flown by with the final sign of her commitment being the sale of her condo, storing her furniture and moving onto the boat full time. Calhoun reciprocated by buying a larger Hatteras, their new 50 ft production sports fisher with a great deal more room as well as a larger power plant enabling a quicker trip anywhere they wanted to go.

They were a couple. For the first time in her life, she felt vulnerable. And truly loved.

"Calhoun, I really am looking forward to getting back to Bimini. It's been too long." The thought of Slayder and his cartoon gang had crossed her mind but had diminished over the past year until now.

Would he still be there? Or perhaps he had moved his operation if he hadn't been busted altogether. All she knew was he had made no attempt to contact her over the last year which suited her fine. "And thanks for doing my dad this favor."

"Not a problem. But I will say it is a most unusual request. A burial at sea."

"I know but Reece had worked for my dad a long time as a dispatcher in dad's trucking company and he always dreamed of going to the ocean but he never got there. With no family of his own, my dad decided the least he could do would be to make sure Reece got to the sea on his final trip."

"Well you sure made Hank nervous."

Nervous was an understatement. Hank took very seriously his duties as captain. Running a boat, maintaining it, fishing, were all fine but he had never had the opportunity to perform a wedding at sea much less a burial. As a devout Catholic he looked upon this sacred trust with all the seriousness it deserved, so much so that he had borrowed a prayer book to make sure he performed this ritual as it should be. He had buried plenty of people's pets at sea, including a couple of his own, but this would be the first time he had the responsibility for human remains, even if they were just ashes.

They had agreed to stop about midway between Bimini and Ft. Lauderdale and scatter Reece's remains at that point. On the way out of Ft. Lauderdale, they managed to pick up a pod of dolphin, at least eight by Hank's count. While it was not unusual to pick up a playful dolphin or two on occasion, these became an informal escort, racing alongside and in front of the Mahalo, surfing off the bow wake, while some performed aerial acrobatics off the stern, much to the delight of everyone on board. Eva decided to go up on the bow and watch this show. She sat with legs dangling over the side hanging onto the handrails which encircled the entire boat. Hank was perched in his customary position on the flying bridge, king of all he surveyed which at the moment was a gentle sea, running about 2-3 feet. There was no land in sight so he knew he was as close to mid-point as dead reckoning would allow. He dropped the throttles back from full speed to neutral in preparation of performing the burial. In doing so, he noticed the Mahalo was sluggish in her response. While they had been out before on this newer version, never had he attempted a crossing before so he shrugged it off. Besides he had a funeral service on his mind. He went ahead and gave one quick blast of the air horn, signaling to Eva it was time for the ceremony. Almost immediately, the dolphin raced away as though somehow, they knew their duty was over.

He slid down the ladder from the flying bridge on his way to his cabin to retrieve his prayer book when the sliding doors to the salon were flung open and with urn in hand and a grunt, Eva slung the urn overboard. His first thought was how did she get to the salon so quickly?

Calhoun had been dozing in one of the fighting chairs and was trying to get his bearings when the urn went sailing past his head and made an audible splash just beyond the stern. He turned to look at Hank, sure that the look of stun and shock he saw in his captain's face was mirrored in his own. The looks on both men were so intense it caused Eva to take a step back.

"Whaaat?" she asked wondering if she was somehow in trouble.

Hank found his voice first. "Eva, do you know what you just did?"

"Yeah, I threw the urn in, wasn't that what I was supposed to do?"

"Honey" Calhoun interjected, "We were supposed to say a few words then *scatter* the ashes."

"Ohh," Eva responded.

And with that both Calhoun and Hank erupted into great peals of laughter. The anxiety Hank had been feeling all day had vanished and with an audible sigh he let go of the tension accompanying it.

"Well, at least you saved me from performing my first real burial at sea so I guess that is some consolation."

"Nothing more we can do here" Calhoun said. "Let's get going, Bimini awaits. And Eva, when my time comes, please *scatter* my ashes. I don't want to spend eternity feeling like some genie in a bottle sitting on the ocean floor."

Hank bounded back up the ladder to the flying bridge and pushed the throttles full forward from the neutral position they had been in. The Mahalo should have responded by leaping out of the sea. Instead she could not even plane out. She was dragging severely. Something was wrong.

Hank immediately pulled the throttles back and returned both engines to neutral.

Calhoun had noticed his boat was not responding as it should but before he could turn around in his fighting chair to pose the question, Hank was already past him saying “I’m not sure boss. I’m going to check the engine room.”

Hank disappeared inside. Unlike the previous boat where you gained access by duckwalking through a small passage, this newer version had an access door large enough to enter with only having to bend over slightly. He flipped on the light switch just inside the door revealing a pair of 275-hp Lincoln V-8 diesels. He was not prepared for the sight that greeted him. Eva had trailed in behind him and gasped when she took in the scene. The engine room was filling with water and more gushing in. It was obvious the bilge pumps either were not working or could not keep up with the volume of water filling the engine compartment.

“What does this mean Hank?”

Trying to cover the growing concern in his voice he turned and looked Eva straight in the eye.

“It means, Eva, the Mahalo is sinking.”

Chapter 13

Eva immediately spun around to go grab Calhoun while Hank sloshed further into the engine room to try and determine the source of the leak.

Calhoun raced to the engine room and was heartsick over what he saw but kept his wits about him.

"Hank, should we call in a Mayday?"

"I was thinking about that. Go ahead and call Miami Station and have them stand by. In the meantime, I'm going to try and determine why we are taking on so much water and why the pumps aren't handling it."

Calhoun shot Hank a worried look. "Captain, the water is almost to the batteries. I already see some electrical arching over there. Best you get on your life vest like we practiced and let's abandon ship just as we have rehearsed. This is just a boat. It can be replaced, you can't."

"Boss, you may be right but I have never lost a boat yet and I don't intend to start now." And with that he turned and plunged deeper in the compartment.

Hank had drilled both Calhoun and Eva on what to do in case of an emergency so Calhoun immediately dashed back up the stairs into the main salon where the radio was located.

He almost got sick as he uttered words he never imagined he would say.

"MAYDAY! MAYDAY! Miami Coast Guard this is the Mahalo, Whiskey Zulu Yankee one four four nine approximately 25 miles east of your location on a heading for Bimini, we are taking on water and may need assistance."

"Mahalo, this is Coast Guard Station, Miami. Roger that. We will have a helo standing by. Please keep apprised. Copy?"

"Copy, Miami."

With that, Calhoun had done all he could do other than put on a life vest and stand by the raft he had just pulled up from the stern locker. It was up to Hank now as to the fate of the Mahalo.

Even though this engine room was larger than on the original Mahalo, the quarters were still tight. Hank had seen bubbles erupting near the stern indicating the location of the leak but he still had no idea as to its cause. He prayed it was not a hull breach as there was nothing he could do about that but he was confident he had not hit anything so a breach was unlikely. Even though he had been on a fiberglass boat for a couple of years now he still held a deep-seated mistrust of this new composite material. "Give me a wooden hull anytime," he thought. He knew he would have to work fast, not only due to the flow of unstoppable water but the heat in the engine room thrown off by the twin diesels meant he could only stay for a very few minutes without risking passing out from the heat contained in these tight quarters.

As he neared the stern, he spotted the cause of the problem. These engines were water cooled and one of the clamps on an intake hose had come loose. Rather than recirculating through the engine, the water was pumping directly into the boat. It took Hank a few minutes to reattach the hose and tighten the clamp and none too soon as the water was precariously close to the batteries and he knew nothing conducted electricity better than salt water and he sure did not want to be knee deep in it if the batteries started to short out. He scurried out of the engine room but waited just outside of the door to ensure the bilge pumps were now doing their job.

Calhoun and Eva looked at him from the salon wearing their life vests and worried looks with equal discomfort. "Miami has our position and is standing by" reported Calhoun.

"We should be ok" Hank reassured him as he grabbed a dishtowel from the galley to mop the sweat from his face and neck as a result of the time he had been in the choking heat of the confined space now vacated. "I fixed the source of the leak; it was a lose clamp on an intake hose. I will have someone look at it when we get to Bimini but for now, I'm going to change out of these drenched clothes while the pumps get rid of this water weight, then we can get underway. Shouldn't take us an hour or so to get to the island." And with that he disappeared into the crew's quarters.

"And I think I'll have a double scotch and water," Calhoun said. "It's been a helluva trip already and we are only half way there and on our first day to boot. What else awaits?"

"I'll join you in that drink, Calhoun." said Eva. "A little bracer is just what the doctor ordered!"

Chapter 14

Calhoun and Eva settled into the stern fighting chairs to enjoy their drinks, the sun and each other's company. Eva grew more animated the closer they got to Bimini. Calhoun could not help but wonder why she was becoming increasingly more nervous.

"Eva, what is wrong? You have not been this agitated since I've known you."

"I dunno, perhaps it's the fact we are back in Bimini and Slayder could be here. We've had such a great year with no interference from him. It's been almost too quiet from him for my way of thinking. Then the boat almost sinking. Just a lot of stuff running through my head."

Calhoun thought for a minute and said "Nothing I can do about Slayder. He's either here or not and we'll just have to handle that situation as it arises. As far as the boat, we'll be tied up at The Big Game Club. I know the old saying of 'the place where 90% of boats sink is at the dock' may or not be true but I still feel pretty safe there. But if it makes you feel better, I'll go up topside and ask Hank if he will radio ahead and see if we can get a room at the club or the Compleat Angler so you can sleep on terra firma."

Eva leaned over from her chair and gave Calhoun a lingering kiss. "First of all, giving me that sinking statistic did not help my anxiety one bit. But thanks for trying to get a room. You're the best."

Calhoun scaled the ladder to the bridge and passed his request on to Hank who chuckled over Eva's concern of sinking but immediately got on the radio to see what he could find.

NOTHING!

He could find not a single room on the island. He had forgotten this was the weekend of the Island Fishing Rodeo, where every fish caught, regardless of type, counted in some form or fashion to a boats cumulative point total. The more exotic the fish, like billfish or sharks the higher the points associated with them. There were other classifications as well, such as weight, but suffice it to say since every type of fish counted for something, the tournament attracted a lot of boats and with that a large purse. He had a hell of a time trying to get a slip and only accomplished that due to his long association with Mr. Holmes at the Big Game Club who remembered the huge marlin head they had donated to him a year ago. It also required a 65' Chris Craft Cabin Cruiser to relocate from the dock to an anchorage in the harbor which did not make the members of the yacht, Hanky Panky, very happy.

As they slipped through the jetties and into the harbor, they were immediately overwhelmed by the sheer number of vessels docked and at anchor in the harbor. There were literally scores of boats, of every make and size. Some so small, Calhoun wondered how they could even be able to boat a good-sized fish should they be lucky enough to encounter one. They passed the Hanky Panky on the starboard side as they made their way to the slip she had just vacated, drawing a few stern looks from her crew. But Eva noticed something else unusual about the cabin cruiser. There seemed to be an abundance of scantily clad women on board. In fact, it seemed to her too many for a fishing tournament.

Eva got up from the fighting chair she had been sitting in and made her way to the flying bridge where Hank was about to back into his assigned berth. "Hank, what gives with that boat in the harbor and all the women on board?"

"That is a hooker boat. They tend to follow these big tournaments to accommodate the mostly all male fishing teams that participate in these tourneys."

"I can't believe that but it does explain the name of the boat, I guess."

"Yep. Now Eva let me concentrate on getting this boat backed in here. It's really tight as you can see. I only have about 80' between these docks and since I'm 50' feet and the other boats stick out I gotta be really careful. In fact, how about throwing my stern line to someone I think you may recognize standing on the dock ready to catch it."

She turned and immediately recognized the grin she had not seen in a year…Bones!

Once secured to the dock, Bones hopped on board where there was an abundance of hugs and laughs as the four renewed acquaintances. Hank could not wait to relay the day's events, starting with the tossing of the entire urn to the near sinking of the Mahalo.

"Bones, do you know anyplace I could stay on land tonight?" queried Eva.

"No ma'am. The island has been booked for weeks. Even to the point where some folks are camping on the beach. Hell, as soon as I found out you guys were coming in today it was all I could do to grab a table for you at the Big Game Club which Mr. Holmes helped with. We gotta eat early though so what say I help in washing down the boat and we mosey on over?"

Eva took advantage of having an extra deck hand by going below to take the first shower. She emerged 20 minutes later in shorts and tube top wearing flat sandals. Looking so refreshed inspired Calhoun to take the next shower and he was followed by Hank who came out in his all khaki uniform.

The four sauntered up to the club where they were immediately seated in the main dining room. As in many island restaurants there was a separate dining area for a boat's crew so owners and crew were segregated but due to the number of people on the island for the tournament, those rules were suspended. Over their respective cocktails they further caught up with Bones and news on the island. The good news was that Princess Tanika was back on the island for the tournament and would be performing her famous fire eating show at the Calypso Club for the duration of the tournament. They immediately made plans to catch a show in a couple of days. The bad news for Eva was that Slayder was still around. Doing what, Bones did not know as the guy came and went a lot but Bones was sure he was up to no good. Bones did say the Royal Bahamian Police had brought over extra personnel from Nassau and they had been on Bimini for a while.

He suspected they were trying to discourage whatever activities Slayder and his gang were up to. The question really was how successful were they able to be?

"How do you know they are from Nassau" queried Eva.

"Easy. Our police do not carry guns. These guys? These guys are armed to the teeth like they are ready to start World War III."

Chapter 15

Dinner came and consisted of grilled Wahoo with red rice and conch fritters. However, the news of Slayder and the prospect of sleeping on the boat only served to unnerve Eva further. She decided she wanted to call it an early evening. Since they were not part of the tournament, it was determined they would wait until all of the boats involved were gone then they would leave around eight a.m.

Bones headed home while the other three strolled the dock heading to the Mahalo. Calhoun had his customary pipe clenched between his teeth, a constant wisp of smoke trailing behind him.

Sensing Eva was distraught, he placed a protective arm around her shoulders and pulled her closer to him. "Don't worry about the boat. We will be fine. As far as Slayder is concerned, I doubt he is around, not with all these boats and people here for the tournament. Let's enjoy the week we planned on spending here."

She shook her head in acknowledgment and cuddled in closer to Calhoun. Both of them missed the gleam in Hank's eye and the coy smile on his face.

Once on board, Eva headed straight to their stateroom while Calhoun lingered behind to discuss the next day's schedule. Once satisfied, he went on down to join Eva in their stateroom. She was already in bed trying to read a book but the sound of the waves lapping against the hull had her too nervous to concentrate. Calhoun was brushing his teeth when there came a loud rapping at the door. Eva slipped out of the bed to open the door surprised to find Hank standing there wearing his swim suit along with diving flippers, a dive mask over his face and a snorkel in his mouth holding a five-pound bag of baking potatoes. She immediately broke into giggles at the unseemly sight in front of her.

"Hank, what are you doing and what are those potatoes for?"

"Well, Eva, if you wake up tonight throw one of these potatoes on the floor. If you hear a thud, you know you are alright. However, if you hear a splash…"

"Oh you" and with a playful slap to his arm she closed the door but with a huge grin on her face. Hank's antics had achieved its desired purpose, it had calmed Eva down.

"Calhoun, where did you find such a nutnik?"

"I wish I knew but I'm glad I did."

Chapter 16

No one needed an alarm clock the next morning as the heighted activity along the docks was enough to awaken the heaviest of sleepers. Crews were rigging lines and loading up with ice and other provisions as the participating tournament boats cranked up and made their way slowly out of the harbor and into the great expanse of water on the other side. The head tournament boat was already on station, her multiple flags making it easy to distinguish her. Since this was a shotgun start, no one could go past this boat until the airhorn sounded which would be promptly at 8am. They would fish until 4pm at which time all boats would have to bring in their lines, unless they had previously reported being hooked up with a fish, and make their way back to the Compleat Angler for weighing and tabulating the fish caught that day.

All of this tournament activity meant the Mahalo could take its time leaving since there was no reason to get caught up in the tournament boat traffic. Eva took the extra time to complete her daily routine of 100 brushstrokes through her hair. Calhoun had to admit her hair absolutely glowed as it naturally fell around her shoulders which served only to enhance her beauty.

"It's gonna be a hot one today," Hank announced as both Calhoun and Eva emerged from their room.

Calhoun had on a denim baseball cap along with blue shorts and a white shirt. Eva came out in a bikini which she proudly announced had cost $150 with her hair in its customary pony tail pulled through her baseball cap, this one with a Pier 66 logo on the front. Calhoun could only shake his head in amazement at the price of her suit as the bottom half consisted of nothing more than dental floss attached to a microscopic sized triangle. No need for the top as Eva had long ago served notice, she was not going to wear a top when out on the boat. Hank did not complain but Calhoun had remained chagrined over her decision for several months now. But he knew better than to argue. Hank was decked out in his all khaki uniform and no one knew yet how Bones would be dressed as he was tasked with getting ice and baits and had yet made it to the boat.

"Sunscreen for everyone," ordered Hank. "And extra for you Eva! I have a good idea where the fish are going to be today and where the tournament boats won't be, so hopefully, we will have a good day."

As if on cue, Bones appeared carrying two 50-pound bags of ice along with a bag full of frozen baits. Most folks would crumble under all the weight but it did not seem to have an effect on the well-muscled native.

In a matter of moments, they were underway as Bones put away the ice and the baits and started rigging the lines while Hank maneuvered away from the docks and into the harbor passing the Hanky Panky with more than just a few catcalls coming from this working boat. The strange thing about these whistles was they were coming from the women on the boat directed at the men on the Mahalo. This produced wide grins from Bones and Hank with a stern but playful stare from Eva directed at Calhoun. "Easy there killer," she said. "Don't let this go to your head although I am glad someone else recognizes my good taste!"

Calhoun could only shake his head and wonder what this world was coming to.

Rounding the bend and passing the jetties, the Mahalo was greeted with a vast expanse of very flat ocean liberally sprinkled with dozens of tournament boats working or heading toward their favorite spots. The sun was behind them, sparing them the discomfort of staring into that blinding orb as they made their way out of Bimini but its rays now cooked the cockpit and would continue to do so until they could start their trolling. Hank headed off to the south toward Honeymoon Beach. Since they were really just fishing for fun and perhaps dinner, there really was no pressure to jump right on suspected fishing holes.

Hank leaned over from the fly bridge so he could be better heard by the other three down below.

"I think we will troll over toward Honeymoon Beach. For those of you not familiar with it, it lies about eight miles south of here. Once we get out a little further where this bottom drops off to the shelf below, we should be good to start fishing. Anyway, Honeymoon is shaped like a crescent and known for its pink sands and the fact that it is isolated and mostly uninhabited except for day boats like us. If you guys do your job and catch me some fish, we can cook them on the beach at midday when it's too hot to fish anyway. Once we get there, we'll head toward the leeward side of the island where the anchorage is good and the snorkeling is great.

Now, Bones…get those lines out and stop lollygagging around! We got work to do and mouths to feed!"

The flat ocean was not ideal as Hank would like to see a little wave action which would bring his prey up to the surface. With that said, the flat water today made for ideal conditions to keep an eye on each bait. They had been trolling for about 45 minutes when he saw the surface ripple behind

"ONE…ONE!" Hank yelled, just as the familiar zipzing sound of the line leaving the outrigger resonated through the cockpit. Calhoun jumped up and grabbed his rod from the side cupholder and deftly sat back down, placing it between his legs as he prepared to reel.

"THREE…THREE!" Eva's line next sang out as she gave a quick yelp and with an assist from Bones got her rod jammed into the cup of her chair and hung on as the line roared off the reel, indicating a potentially big fish.

"Remember, Eva, reel as you go down and pull back as far as you can on the way up. Keep that line tight and the pressure constant and you should be okay." Bones turned to look at Hank who was staring at the lines trailing behind. With a shrug of his shoulders and his arms extended palms up, he conveyed to Hank his question.

"Not sure" came the answer from the bridge. "I thought we might have a sail but I think we are in some big dolphin. Let's get those other lines in. Calhoun, do you feel anything on your line?"

As a matter of fact, Calhoun had already determined he had lost his fish and was in the process of bringing his line in as well. With that, he and Bones stood by to give whatever encouragement to Eva they could. Time dragged on as Eva would reel in only to see her efforts go for naught as her fish would make a run and as a result, her line would go screaming off the reel. Ten minutes became twenty and crept toward thirty when it became evident, Eva was growing tired. Calhoun kept trying to keep her spirits up with his words. Barely discernible, Eva began to win the battle as the line stayed on the reel as she brought it in. She turned toward Calhoun, who was sitting in the fighting chair next to her and gave him a determined smile, revealing her deep-set dimples and blazing green eyes. She was still looking at Calhoun when she brought the rod up and the improbable happened. As she pulled the rod back, her hair became entangled in the reel. She was reeling in both the line and her hair until she became face-planted against the reel.

"HELP! HELP!" she screamed, as she realized what she was doing.

Calhoun, try as he might, could not contain himself and doubled over in laughter. The return daggers Eva shot back at him quickly quelled that emotion and just as he started to rise from his seat to help, Hank appeared with scissors in hand. Eva looked up as best she could and as she realized what was about to happen, she screamed, "NOOOO, not my hair!"

SNIP!

Chapter 17

Eva continued to be face-planted against the reel whimpering "no, please no" as tears began to trickle down her cheeks. She had not moved and all she could see from her peripheral vision was Hank standing with scissors in hand.

"Easy Eva, I only cut the line. We lost your fish but your hair is intact. All we need to do is reverse out the reel and free your hair and none of it will be lost."

She wiped her eyes and thanked Hank.

Lost in the confusion was the fact no one had brought in the other two lines contrary to what Hank had requested. They were immediately reminded when the POP and Zipzing echoed in the cockpit.

"Here we go!" yelled Hank. "FOUR! FOUR! Bones, get that rod from Eva and grab four for her. Eva, no time for resting now, there are still fish to be caught!"

Bones handed Eva's rod to Calhoun for him to store while he got the active line to hand off to Eva. He then immediately started to re-rig lines one and three while Eva started reeling at a pace which indicated a much smaller fish. In fact, it was a small dolphin which they kept trailing behind the boat until such time as all lines were in play. They then settled into bailing out the school they were in. As long as one dolphin stayed hooked and trailing behind the boat, the rest of the school tended to follow it and if played correctly, you could catch quite a few, which they did bringing in a total of eight before the school broke off contact. Eva never ceased to marvel at how beautiful dolphin were, full of different shades of blues, greens and yellows. The fish seemingly lit up right before they died displaying all of their hues in one final explosion of color.

"Well, that takes care of lunch and a few other meals" Hank observed as he took one of the fish out to filet and marinate in fresh squeezed lime juice. "I think we are close enough to Honeymoon Beach we should call it a morning and let's get cleaning these fish and enjoy a beach cookout. Everyone agree?"

With the morning they had, all were in agreement and besides the beach seemed to beckon them all.

The Mahalo rounded the point leading into Honeymoon Beach to discover they were the only boat there. With most of the day boats involved in the tournament, they were practically guaranteed to be alone. Hank dropped anchor in about 5 feet of crystal-clear water, deep enough to assure plenty of room beneath the hull but shallow enough to be able to walk the picnic items into the beach.

Once he was certain the anchor had taken hold on the sandy bottom, he dispatched Bones with the grill grate, shovel and charcoal so he could begin to dig the pit for the cookout. Eva and Calhoun were tasked with multiple trips between the Mahalo and shore, carrying coolers and picnic supplies. Once done, Hank dismissed them with strict orders to explore the beach but nor to wander too far as lunch would be ready shortly.

Eva did not need any further encouragement as she grabbed Calhoun's hand and playfully led him over the dunes toward another anchorage on the other side, also quite deserted.

"Have you ever made love in the ocean?" she cooed into Calhoun's ear. The question was so unexpected it caused Calhoun to stammer a no. "Well, let's fix that," as she led him chest deep into the waters where she quickly removed her bikini bottoms and yanked down Calhoun's shorts discovering he was up for the challenge. Floating on her back, she wrapped her legs around his waist and slowly lowered herself onto him.

Later, they lay entangled, sunning themselves on the beach at the edge of the water, fully spent. The sound of an airhorn broke their reverie.

"Lunch," Calhoun said.

"And not a minute too soon" replied Eva. "I'm famished, and I wonder why," giving Calhoun an all-knowing devilish grin. "Let's go!" and with that she leapt up and sprinted toward the dune and the meal waiting on the other side.

Hank was just pulling the dolphin off the grill as they came toward the fire. Also on the fire grate was a pot of beans and rice. On the side was sliced Bimini bread and a chilled bottle of Chardonnay.

"This looks fabulous Hank," Eva proclaimed.

She dug in filling her plate but before she could move too far from the fire Hank yelled, "WAIT!"

It was too late…they had already arrived.

FLIES! Hundreds of black flies seemingly materializing out of thin air. With one hand holding her plate, Eva tried to shoo the pests away by windmilling her free arm around. It was to no avail, there were simply too many of them.

"Eva, run to the water, get about waist deep, they won't follow you that far" Hank instructed.

Like a shot, she was off and as promised the flies did not follow.

"Wow! Where did those come from?" she asked.

"They live in the plants around here until they get a whiff of food then they are everywhere," Hank replied. "I wanted you to wait, I have Sterno cans when lit seem to keep them away. For some reason they hate those fumes."

He finished lighting the handful of Sterno cans and placed them around the perimeter of the fire, allowing enough space for everyone to sit. Eva returned from the water, sitting next to Calhoun who poured her a glass of wine.

"I feel like a castaway," Eva said. "Kinda like our own version of Gilligan's Island, only better."

"Well, you are a damn sight better looking than the movie star and Hank is far better than that captain and Bones damn sure has more sense than Gilligan. Guess that leaves me playing the part of Thurston Howell!" Calhoun chuckled as he made the impromptu comparison. "Hey, since we are on no schedule, why don't we spend a few minutes later on snorkeling?"

"Great idea," Eva said. "Once everyone is through, let's get this stuff back to the boat and fetch the snorkeling gear."

They reversed the order of the way they had off loaded supplies, carrying dirty dishes and empty coolers back to the boat while Bones buried the charcoal coals after dousing them with sea water to make sure they were out.

Once everything was secured, Eva joined Calhoun on the bow to help bring the anchor in. Before they could begin there was a growing roar, forcing everyone to turn and stare back toward the entrance into the anchorage. A huge commercial fishing boat was just rounding the corner.

“What flag is it flying Calhoun?” Eva asked.

“That’s a Cuban flag and that is apparently a Cuban fishing boat. And that’s not all.”

For standing on the bow of the boat was none other than Slayder.

Chapter 18

If there was a contest for most surprised, it would have been difficult to judge who won. Eva's hand flew to her mouth in an involuntary gesture and gasp of shock while Slayder's tan face went from red to burgundy in a rage of recognition. Hank immediately recognized the situation for what it was and was instantly on the radio to the dockmaster at the Big Game Club summoning reinforcements. He only hoped they would be in time.

The dockmaster at the Big Game Club was Tom Millard who had seen his share of trouble over time as a Vietnam Vet even to the point of losing an arm in that conflict. He could discern who was in real trouble or not from a radio call. From the urgency in Hank's voice, he could tell his long-time friend was in trouble. He called up to the police barracks, really little more than a one room building which could accommodate 8 bunks and a bathroom shower combo. It was currently occupied by six of Her Majesty's finest drug interdiction forces. He explained the situation to the captain in charge and before he could hang up, the force was on the move to the docks to board their 35-foot swift boat loaded with electronic gear, two 50 caliber machine guns and powered by three 350 horse powered outboard MercCruisers. If the weight of the motors did not sink the boat, it would make it damn near fly and today, it flew!

Everyone had a specific task on this team, so while the helmsman ignored all no wake courtesies, roaring out of the harbor at full speed and setting course for Honeymoon Beach, the radioman was getting in touch with the US Coast Guard requesting assistance in the form of a helicopter which was immediately airborne and which had a pretty good chance of beating the police to the Mahalo. Two men manned the respective 50 calibers, loaded them and once clear of the harbor fired a few test rounds to make sure they would be ready if called upon. The captain and navigator stood by.

Hank had calmly placed the microphone back in its clip after the call to Bimini. He reached down to grab the only weapon he had on the bridge, the orange flare gun. He called down to Bones to help get the anchor up and instructed both Calhoun and Eva to get inside the main salon. He had no intention of allowing Slayder and friends to board his boat by sitting still. Problem was, the Cuban boat, just by its sheer size, blocked his only exit point. Since Honeymoon Beach was a crescent shaped cay there was only one way in and out and that was further reduced by the shallow bottom.

"Well, Eva. Long time. Why don't you come over and lets you and me catch up!" yelled Slayder.

"Fuck off!" was the response from the cockpit where she and Calhoun stood, ignoring Hank's earlier order. Calhoun could not help but smile at her bravado. She had more moxie than any woman he had ever known.

Slayder broke into a grin while behind him there was movement, Tom and Jerry appeared, each armed with a pistol of some sort.

"I hardly believe you are in any position to be rude and…"

Before he could finish, Hank had gunned the throttles forward causing the Mahalo to shoot in front of the Cuban boat barely missing a collision but ending up changing his position from the starboard side to the port side and putting him in a better place to try to get through the narrow opening leading to the sea. Hank knew he still did not have enough depth to get by without grounding the Mahalo, an option with no options. He was just trying to buy time until help arrived but time was quickly running out

There was laughter from the Cuban boat as its crew seemed to enjoy this game of cat and mouse. Whoever was in the wheelhouse put the boat in reverse closing what little escape passage that may have been open. "Check and mate" thought Hank.

Skimming just 50 feet above the ocean to avoid detection, the Coast Guard Bell helicopter was screaming in toward Bimini at a little more that 150mph. The 80-foot long fishing trawler with its radio masts and outriggers up was the tallest point around so it was easy to make a visual on it. Coming in this low, it was doubtful the copter had been detected yet, which was the whole point. The boat got larger in the windscreen the closer they got, until they were nearly on top of it when the pilot pulled back on the collective causing the orange and white painted calvary to leap up, barely missing the radio mast on the trawler.

Involuntarily, everyone on the Cuban boat ducked while hurrahs erupted from the Mahalo. Slayder whipped around to glare at Eva and the Mahalo, simultaneously wondering how the Coast Guard got here knowing they had to get out quick before they found themselves boxed in. Just at that moment the "fisherman" manning the radar shouted a boat was heading their way and fast. Whoever was maneuvering the Cuban boat knew his business as he whipped the boat around and had it headed back out to sea.

Hank noticed the name on the stern, Revolucion but before he could consider the implications of that name, the sound of machine gun fire interrupted his thoughts. The balance of the calvary had arrived and was making its presence known while the Coast Guard helicopter hovered above the fishing trawler in what could only be considered front row seats to the action unfolding below it.

By the time the Mahalo came out of Honeymoon Beach, the Cuban trawler was at a dead stop and was being boarded by the Royal Bahama interdiction force. On board, 100 bales of marijuana were discovered as well as several unregistered weapons. Slayder and his gang were taken into custody while the Cuban nationals were released as the Bahamas did not want an incident to occur between their country and Cuba. After giving statements, the Mahalo group headed back toward The Big Game Club. No one was any longer interested in snorkeling and all on board were ready for a drink…or several.

Chapter 19

"Whew!" Any one of them could have expressed that sentiment but this time it came from Eva.

They were back at their berth, securely tied up and the boat washed down and all were on their second drink as no one could recall gulping down the first one.

"Well, that takes care of Slayder and the Cartoon Gang" said Eva.

"True, although I will feel better when the US Marshalls get here tomorrow and get them all off the island. I've never seen the jail on Bimini but I can't imagine it's much." Calhoun replied.

"Well, I have seen it, mostly as a holding area for too many rum and Cokes and you are right, it is not meant to hold anyone who is intent on getting out. Although we are on an island so not too many places to run if they did get out" Bones volunteered.

"Okay, everyone, before we get too far down that path, remember we have tickets tonight to the Calypso Club and Princess Tanika. That should be just the thing to get our minds off of today. By the way, anyone notice that ASAP is leading the tournament? They got into the dolphin like we did and added a sail on top of that along with a couple of 'cuda. Good day for them," Hank said.

"As Soon As Possible? Cute name" said Eva.

"It would be but in this case it stands for Always Say A Prayer. Which is an even better name," Hank informed them. "Now let's get moving to shower and get on up to the tip of the island. Bones, you just meet us there."

The steel drum band could be heard halfway across the island as they made their way down the hardpacked earthen street. Tiki torches illuminated their way as they drew closer. For this evening's frivolity, Eva had chosen a scant tie dyed mini-skirt which barely covered her finely shaped rear. Calhoun wore a sky-blue shirt with white shorts and his ever-present pipe clinched between his teeth. Hank remained in a clean khaki shirt and shorts. Bones was dressed like most of the natives, in their Sunday finest as having Princess Tanika on the island was a big deal and not everyone got a chance to see her.

They were seated at a round four top one row back from the stage/dancefloor. The band was doing its job of getting everyone ready with their renditions of Yellow Bird, Guantanamera, Brown Eyed Girl, the famous Day-O (Banana Boat Song) and Your Daddy Ain't Your Daddy (But Your Daddy Don't Know) as well as other island favorites featuring music by a new artist, Bob Marley, along with a mixture of other top 20 tunes. After a Planters Punch on top of the two hearty poured glasses of wine she had consumed on the boat, Eva was ready to dance. Giving Calhoun no option, she dragged him onto the floor where she swayed rhythmically to the island sounds while grinding into Calhoun. It was a sensation he certainly did not mind! As with most Calypso Bands, there was a good deal of freelance playing so a song which normally took 3 minutes lasted easily twice that long. By the time it ended, both Eva and Calhoun were drenched, the ceiling fans doing not much good in the palm frond roofed tiki lounge which was The Calypso Club.

No sooner had they returned to the table than the MC announced it was time for "The one, the only, fire breathing Princess from parts unknown, PRINCESS TANIKA!"

To catcalls and wild applause she entered from stage left. Painted from head to toe in silver, ala Goldfinger, she ran onto the stage, topless, gyrating to the music. What followed was 45 minutes of fire eating, singing and audience participation. Calhoun swore she was the prettiest girl on the island next to Eva, an observation fueled by his companion Johnny Walker but not totally without merit.

Once the show ended, many in the audience headed home, for tomorrow was the final day of the tournament. A second show was also scheduled for that night which promised to be wilder than the first. The Mahalo crew, exhausted by their day, decided to call it quits as well. Calhoun excused himself in order to use the men's room prior to the long walk, promising to meet up with everyone outside.

He stood at the urinal, softly whistling one of the evenings songs when he felt, more than saw, a presence next to him at the adjoining urinal. Trying to be discreet, he turned his head slightly only to be confronted by the one, the only, Princess Tanika! The princess was no princess at all! She was a he!

Implants and all! Calhoun had been ogling her all night. And to make matters worse, the Princess asked in the deepest of baritones, "Did you enjoy the show?" Gone was the falsetto voice he had listened to just minutes earlier. Gone was his voice as well as the shock of seeing her in the men's room had literally left him speechless. All he could do was nod his head in the affirmative, zip up, quickly wash his hands and flee to his crew waiting patiently on him outside. When he shared with them what had just occurred, they all erupted in great spams of laughter, tears running down all of their faces. Calhoun could scarcely see the humor in it but later did admit it was rather funny. It was, in fact, the perfect way to end the day.

Chapter 20

The day dawned with the sky full of reds, pinks and bright oranges. Eva found Hank on the flying bridge, his face frozen in a scowl, studying the horizon.

"Good Morning Captain," she chirped. "What a glorious and beautiful morning!"

"I don't like it one bit!" came the reply. In the background, engines were firing up as boats made their way out of the harbor for the final day of the tournament.

"Why, Hank? Look at that sky!"

"That sky is exactly why I don't like it. Have you ever heard of 'Red in morning, sailors take warning'? It's an old seaman's diddly which is accurate more often than not. Means we may have some weather moving in. I've been listening to Miami weather; they are tracking a tropical depression which seems to be moving in our direction."

"So, what is our plan then?"

"The plan is to go back toward Honeymoon Beach and get that snorkeling in we missed yesterday. We can troll there to see if we can catch anything. No need to rush back to Lauderdale as the storm system is still a couple of days out if it doesn't change course."

Lopping down the dock came Bones with a fifty-pound bag of ice slung over his shoulder and carrying a couple of bags of mullet for the days fishing. "Weather coming Captain!" he announced as he drew closer.

"I can see that! Let's get that stuff stored away so we can get underway. I think we will troll toward the concrete ship."

"Yes sir!"

Coming up the stairs to the bridge with his perpetual smoke ring from his pipe came a shirtless Calhoun.

"So, I overheard we are heading to the concrete ship. Since we never got a chance to discuss it, tell me about it."

As Bones threw off the spring lines followed by the bow and stern lines, Hank settled into the Captain's chair.

"As you saw yesterday that skeleton of a ship is the remains of the S.S. Sapona, better known to the locals as the concrete ship. She was built in 1920 by the Liberty Ship Building Company over in Wilmington, North Carolina. She was first used to store oil and later stored whiskey during Prohibition. Not sure how that mixture worked out but anyway, she ended up here as a result of a hurricane when she ran aground on a reef which caused the stern to break off. The Navy and Air Force used her as target practice during World War Two. Being an old Navy guy, we learned about it while I was enlisted so don't go think I have every tidbit memorized around here 'cause I don't. Other than that. Now it's time for you two to get downstairs and man your fighting chairs."

By the time the two descended, Bones already had their lines out and was busy making up other baits.

Calhoun looked toward the north where most of the tournament boats were now underway from their shotgun start, trying to be the first to arrive at their favorite fishing hole. No one was heading in their direction since this area was not really known for an abundance of fish. That thought had barely crossed his mind when Hank yelled out "ONE!" and immediately followed that by "THREE" as both Calhoun's and Eva's lines snapped out of the clips holding them to the outriggers.

"Dolphin" came his answer to the unasked question.

And it seemed they were hooked into the king of all dolphin as no matter how hard they tried, they could not make any headway into getting their fish closer to the boat. It seemed as though as soon as one of them got their fish close, it would immediately go spooling back out again only to have the process repeat itself with the other angler. This went on for 15 minutes forcing Hank to place both engines in neutral. Now he had a decision to make; continue to sit in idle gear and allow a fair fight or back down on the fish, reducing both anglers to doing little more than just reeling in their respective quarry. Looking at how tired both Calhoun and Eva were becoming, he realized this time the fish had the upper hand so he put the boat in reverse and yelled out "Reel, reel hard!"

Reel they did but the result remained the same, one angler would make headway only to lose what line they had gained while the other angler made progress.

Without warning a huge explosion of laughter erupted from the flying bridge.

"You guys are hooked into the same fish" Hank shouted. "Bones, cut Eva's line, she has fouled hooked Calhoun's fish in the tail. Seems the reason you guys were struggling so much is you were both working at cross purposes bringing in that dolphin broadside to the boat. But it is a good-sized fish, I'd say 30 pounds or so." Just like the day before, by the time they had boated the fish they were right on top of Honeymoon Beach so they repeated the same steps of dropping anchor and ferrying supplies to the beach for another cookout, this time assuredly without Cuban company. Rather than repeat their dalliance from yesterday, both Calhoun and Eva returned to the boat after lunch where they donned fins and masks and leisurely backflipped off of the Mahalo … right into a school of barracuda. Calhoun would have levitated right out of the water if he could have but he was damn certain he could walk on water to get away from this predicament for as he looked in all directions all he could see were teeth. He knew these sleek, bullet shaped scavengers were lighting quick. How they had not seen this school before going over the side was a mystery but nonetheless, they were surrounded. Before he could figure out how to get back on board, Eva nonchalantly started swimming toward the Sapona and as a result, the barracuda moved on, leaving them alone.

"Don't let the little things bother you Calhoun" she said as she looked over her shoulder toward her still rattled companion. All he could do was shake his head in amazement and follow in her wake.

The abundance of marine life around the Sapona was startling, thus answering why barracuda were in the area. There were too many fish to recognize but Calhoun did note one good sized grouper lurking about. He was admiring it when suddenly Eva grabbed his arm startling him in the process. She grunted through her snorkel and pointed to the bottom of the ship where a long line of lobsters were coming out of their hiding places and were seemingly marching toward deeper water. The brown ribbon of crustaceans were oblivious to the presence of the couple floating above them and were foregoing the hiding places where they normally dwelled to keep away from predators.

Eva rolled on her back, taking the snorkel out so she could talk.

"What the hell is going on? There must be dozens of those things leaving every nook and cranny of that ship. It's eerie."

"I don't know but let's get back and let Hank know what we just saw. He may have an explanation for us."

A few minutes later they were back on board the Mahalo. Hank listened intently to the scene Eva described. When she finished, he looked more concerned than ever that day. "The storm is going to be worse than we thought."

"How can you possibly know that and what does that have to do with a bunch of lobsters?"

"It's the barometric pressure. It's dropping, lobsters sense it and are heading toward deeper waters for safety. I've heard of these parades but never witnessed one so consider yourselves fortunate from that standpoint. Let's get this cookout cleaned up and then I would suggest we head back to Bimini to learn what we can about this weather.

Chapter 21

Despite the beautiful day, a certain gloom had settled over the crew of the Mahalo. Would they be leaving Bimini before their scheduled departure? Part of that question was answered by the line of boats waiting to take on fuel at one of the three fuel docks on the island. It was obvious they were not the only ones worried about the weather but given the line of vessels for fuel, it made better sense to go tie up and call the dockmaster to reserve a time slot to take on diesel. Hank was told the tournament had been called early with the TICA out of Georgetown, South Carolina being the winning boat.

"TICA?" asked Eva. "And that no doubt has a meaning too."

"I know the owner. Jack is a great guy. It stands for This I Can't Afford. And knowing Monica, his wife, that boat is not the only thing he can't afford" grinned Calhoun.

His answer brought a laugh from Eva who was still chuckling when she looked up and saw the captain of the interdiction force walking with long purposeful strides toward the Mahalo. His face was a mask of emotion so Eva called out to him "Coming to tell us goodbye now that you caught those smugglers?"

"I wish I could. Unfortunately, I have some bad news." Before anyone could ask, he continued. "It's Slayder. He's escaped."

Chapter 22

"You had better come aboard and tell us what happened" Hank suggested. Once they were all settled in the main salon, the captain offered up what he knew.

"Since we had prisoners in the jail, which is a rare occurrence on these outlying islands with the exception of drunks, we posted two men to watch over them last night.

One of them, my sergeant major, was handling the interrogation of the two known as Tom and Jerry leaving one of the local officers to watch over this Slayder fella. Anyway, the local left his post to go use the restroom, or so he says, and when he returned, Slayder was gone. Someone had gotten the skeleton key for the entire building and had let him go. Whether this was an inside job, we don't know. My force, along with the local police searched door to door last night and this morning, especially in Baileys Town. There are simply not that many places you can hide on this island but he is nowhere to be found. I believe he got in touch with his buddies on that Cuban fishing vessel and they sent a dingy to pull him off the island.

It's a shame the U.S. Marshalls that had planned on picking up all three could not get in here last night but we thought we were secure. We did get the other two culprits to talk in exchange for a possible plea bargain. Apparently, you guys busted up a sizeable operation on the day of your picnic at Honeymoon Beach. Their intention was to dump and hide those marijuana bales on South Bimini and have them picked up that night by a DC 3 which was scheduled to land after midnight. You may not know this, but most airstrips are laid out according to the prevailing winds in the area. Not here. Here, we lay them out according to how much land we need with prevailing winds a secondary consideration. Sometimes that makes for some interesting take offs and landings. Anyway, since so few people live over there and the airfield is uncontrolled, they pretty much had the place to themselves for the loading operation. From there they were heading somewhere in the Okeechobee Swamp area over in Florida to drop off the haul.

They also volunteered this: it seems this Slayder is still pretty pissed over being abandoned by Miss Eva. Vows he will get his revenge as he has taken it personally. For that reason, I'm going to post two men down here tonight but I would suggest you may want to consider going back to the states in the morning."

"We were considering that anyway, given the weather" Calhoun said. "Now I think this pretty much cinches it."

"The U.S. Marshalls will be here in the morning to pick up those other two. Knowing what I know about drug smuggling into Florida, I don't think you will have to worry about those two for a while" responded the Captain as he stood to leave the Mahalo. "Good Luck."

Hank saw the policeman off the boat and by the time he returned he was getting a call over the radio from the dockmaster letting him know he could come get fuel between 8 and 8:15 tonight. This meant they would be staying at least one more night as no one wanted to cross in the dark unnecessarily. Hank was also informed the storm was gaining speed and heading toward South Florida. They would be safer tied up at Pier 66 so the decision was made to leave at first light. Since there were a couple of hours before their scheduled fuel time, they wandered off the boat heading to the Red Lion, leaving Bones to stand watch.

"Calhoun, I don't know how you can pack so much adventure into such a short period of time but somehow you manage" mused Eva. "Living with you is literally a thrill a minute."

"Remember, you brought this Slayder guy into our lives" Calhoun retorted.

"Actually, he brought you into mine so I guess I should be thankful" she replied.

As the three of them strolled toward the Red Lion it was difficult not to notice the number of young women filling the street. "Hanky Panky girls" observed Hank. "The tournament is over and they are trying to make what they can off who they can tonight as they no doubt will be leaving with the rest of us tomorrow."

As if on cue, the women began soliciting everyone they passed and made no secret about their purpose asking every eligible looking man if he would like a 'date'. Eva was incensed while Hank and Calhoun were amused. The only thing saving them all from a heated discussion amongst themselves was their arrival at the Red Lion.

Woody greeted them at the door and was disappointed to learn they would be heading out early the next day.

"You guys are quite the legend on the island what with the drug bust and all." Woody said. "Although I did hear one got away. Hard to figure how he kept from being recaptured on this island."

None of the Mahalo gang were interested in pursuing that particular conversation which Woody picked up on immediately. "Well, tonight we have to start, fresh caught Stone Crab Claws, followed by Red Snapper Almondine along with peas and rice. Enjoy!"

They made small talk while they ate. The disbelief Slayder was once again on the loose and with some kind of twisted motivation for payback on Eva for his perception of their relationship was beyond understanding.

"You can't win an argument with an ignorant man" Calhoun reminded her. "How you saw your relationship and how he saw it are obviously two vastly different viewpoints. What I can't figure is why he is still holding onto this fantasy especially since it has been over a year since you guys last saw one another."

"He is crazy, plain and simple" was all Eva could offer.

While they were debating the merits of long defunct relationships, two anglers from the tournament sauntered in with a couple of the working girls off the Hanky Panky and headed toward the bar.

“Speaking of relationships, there are a couple of short term ones I bet will work out just fine” quipped Hank. “Their boat is going to have to change anchorage tonight as I heard Chalks has at least two flights coming in early tomorrow to get passengers off the island before the storm hits and they need the landing space. With several boats making a dash back to Miami tonight, they can probably find dock space.”

“Probably so” said Calhoun. “I tell you what, now that we have just wolfed down this meal, let’s try some of their house made Key Lime Pie and head back to the boat so we can let Bones go home.” Hearing no dissension, they finished the meal with the house dessert, paid the tab bidding Woody adieu in the process and started strolling back toward their berth.

Chapter 23

They had just turned onto the docks which gave an unencumbered view straight to the harbor where the Hanky Panky along with several other boats lay anchored when they were met with the sound of an explosion. WHOOSH! WHOOM! Right before their eyes the Hanky Panky lifted slightly out of the water before settling back and rapidly becoming engulfed in flames.

"What the…" uttered a shocked Eva. Hank was off on a dead run yelling for everyone to get to their runabouts and get to the harbor to assist everyone on board the distressed yacht.

By the time Hank got to the Mahalo, Bones was already gone having hijacked an adjacent yacht's seventeen-foot Boston Whaler and made his way to the now flaming Hanky Panky. He had picked up eight survivors and was coming back toward the dock to drop them so he could continue his rescue efforts. By now, the entire harbor was alive with small boats, skiffs and runabouts heading toward the blaze. The fraternity of yachtsmen were all involved in saving what they could for a fellow seaman. The challenge now was to rescue all souls and get them away, for it was obvious they could do nothing for the stricken vessel. Without a fireboat to spray water on the flames, which Bimini did not have, they were reduced to being spectators to the conflagration once known as the Hanky Panky.

The armada of rescue boats made it difficult to get close to those in the water without risking the possibility of running over the very people they were trying to save. Additionally, they needed to gather everyone pulled from the Hanky Panky in one place if they were going to have any chance at an accurate headcount to determine if anyone was missing.

As it turned out, the nearest dock to the unfolding tragedy was where the Mahalo was tied up. By default, Hank, Eva and Calhoun found themselves assisting in gathering up the rescued, taking names and rendering what assistance they could. What caused the sudden explosion was without question for the sound gave away the origin, a sound every captain dreaded to hear.

Apparently, one of the crew had attempted to start the engines in preparation to move the boat to a slip at the Compleat Angler in order to make way for the early arrival of Chalks Airlines in the morning. However, he had failed to vent the engine compartment prior to starting the engines, an absolute requirement on gas powered boats like the Hanky Panky. Without proper venting, any spark created by starting the engine can and often does create a gas vapor - induced explosion just like the one that had occurred. There is not much anyone can do as the resultant explosion tends to overtake any efforts to quell the flames, the result being a substantial if not total loss of the boat. The Hanky Panky had in no time burned to the waterline where it put itself out from lack of anything left to burn.

Thankfully, the interdiction force was still on the island as they were not scheduled to leave until the next day. They took control of the scene, ushering all survivors inside a meeting area at the Big Game Club, providing blankets to those who needed them despite the tropical temperatures, getting a headcount and deciding next steps. Fortunately, no one was seriously injured or burned, a miracle in itself. Since all hotel rooms on the island were still booked due to the tournament, it was decided the Freedom Hall at the local AME Church would be used for everyone to bunk in.

An hour or so later, Hank caught up with the captain of the interdiction force to determine if there was anything the Mahalo could do, knowing full well it was unlikely.

"Thank you, Hank, but no. We have reached out to the U.S. Coast Guard to send a cutter to help us tow the Hanky Panky out of the harbor before the storm hits and she ends up sinking where she is. We will have to process the 15 people off of the boat as they lost everything except for the customers who scampered back to where they were staying after we got through interviewing them. The rest, without passports, which were lost in the fire, will have to wait. We appreciate all of your efforts and especially the quick thinking on your mates' part to get on scene as fast as he did to start pulling people out of the water. It's been a terrible night but we are blessed no lives were lost."

Having overheard the report from the police captain, Calhoun, Eva, Hank and Bones turned to leave as there was nothing left for them to do there.

They reassembled on the deck outside of the meeting hall. Hank told Bones he should go on home and thanked him for his contributions to the rescue effort, and informing him since it was past their refueling appointment, they would have to take care of that bit of business in the morning. Eva, Calhoun and Hank all said goodbye to Bones with hugs and promises to return to the island soon.

As the three started back toward the Mahalo, Calhoun started to chuckle.

"What could you possibly find amusing at a time like this?" asked Eva.

"Well, I just remember that old line about being nervous as a whore in church. Seems there will be a lot of nerves tonight with that group since they are all staying at the AME Church Hall!"

Eva playfully slapped at Calhoun's arm, then took it and wrapped it around her.

"You are terrible. Let's just go home."

And the next morning they did just that.

PART TWO

Chapter 24

Two Years Later: Summer 1969

It was difficult to believe how quickly two years had flown by since that fateful weekend in Bimini which saw a major drug bust take place along with the destruction of the Hanky Panky. Not to mention a hurricane. They had awakened that morning and left among numerous squalls, one of which produced a sizeable water spout. For a few moments, they were forced to outrun and outmaneuver the spout as it seemed to chase them. Yet they made it back to Pier 66 a scant 36 hours before Hurricane Abby had slammed into Cuba causing major flood damage then turned its sights on South Florida where those same torrential rains came accompanied with a handful of spin off tornados for good measure.

Calhoun and Eva had ridden out the storm securely berthed at Pier 66 but it had been so uncomfortable and a bit traumatic they had decided to become landlubbers as well, by purchasing a condo and felt fortunate to find one which met their needs back at Bahia Mar where Eva had initially lived. Their lives had been idyllic, with the exception of a few visits by the Miami Narcotics Division who were trying to get a bead on Slayder. There was no question drugs were becoming more of a problem in the area and Slayder had been identified as one of the operatives responsible for the increased traffic. Eva and Calhoun had also been warned that their inadvertent drug bust two years ago outside of Honeymoon Beach had cost Slayder dearly monetarily and, according to a couple of informants, he was still focused on exacting his revenge on the two of them.

"Well Calhoun, hard to believe how much time has gone by since our last trip to the Bahamas. I now realize how much I have missed it." said Eva. She was in the midst of packing for a planned three week fishing/cruising trip as she spoke to Calhoun who was seated comfortably on the balcony off of the master bedroom overlooking the marina. Snickerdoodle had taken up his now customary residency on his lap. "Not to shortchange our trips to the Ocean Reef Club. I love Key Largo. I enjoy Marathon and our day trips to Key West for the sightseeing and especially the bar hopping. But at the end of the day, they aren't the Bahamas. Besides, we need to check in on Bones and the entire gang down there."

"Are you sure you do not want to fly in and just meet Hank and the boat? "asked Calhoun. "You do remember we have to tow a seventeen foot Boston Whaler over there that one of Bones' cousins has purchased?"

"No way!" came the quick response. "We need to stick together. But I do like the idea of changing our luck by not staying again at the Big Game Club. I think the marina at the Compleat Angler will be perfect, especially since we kinda met there."

"Yeh, Hank was going to call the wireless operator on Bimini and have her contact Bones so we could coordinate his schedule with ours and get the latest news from the island. I'm looking forward to staying at the Compleat Angler too. I like Mrs. Duncombe, the owner. I'm glad she was convinced to open her home up as a rooming house by Captain Stank Wood out of Miami. He convinced her and then he convinced his captain friends to stay there and now look at the place and how it has grown into a full-fledged inn!"

"And I love her sign hanging over the entryway to the dining room. 'Shorts for breakfast, shorts for lunch, oh but not for dinner'. She brought a bit of her English decorum to the island."

"Well, if you will stop gabbing and finish packing, we can get on our way. What do you need with all that stuff anyway? You stay in a bikini, with little or no fabric. Hell, all I take is basically a day bag."

"That's the difference between men and women Calhoun. And if you need me to, I can show you some other differences, just come over here."

Chapter 25

Between finishing packing, getting a refresher course in the difference between men and women and the normal three hour, which had taken better than six, boat ride to Bimini, Hank, Calhoun and Eva did not arrive until well after dusk. They had run into a bit of a problem while towing the Whaler. Calhoun had been sleeping in his customary fighting chair when Hank noticed one of the gauges indicated an engine was running hot. He motioned for Eva to come to the bridge. "Looks like I have something going on with the port engine. Take the bridge, and keep a lookout. I'm going down to the engine room and take a look. She is on automatic pilot so all you have to do is stay alert."

"Got it" was her quick reply.

Hank disappeared off the bridge heading toward the engine room where he was gone for forty-five minutes. When he came back, he found Eva staring intently straight ahead.

"Everything ok Captain?"

"I can't find anything so we may have nothing more than a faulty gauge. But Eva, did you notice anything while I was gone?" With that, he stepped to the side to give Eva a view of the ocean behind them.

Then it hit her, the Whaler was gone and nowhere in sight.

"Oh my God" she screamed loud enough to awaken Calhoun who jumped up looking for whatever had caused that reaction from her.

"Mr. Hipp," announced Hank "the tow line has snapped and somewhere behind us is the Whaler. If you would bring the line in, I'm going to circle back."

Calhoun acknowledged the plan by bringing in the rope as Hank turned the boat around. His first search pattern was to head straight back down the heading they had been on. After an hour of that with no luck, he started to widen his search taking into account the currents and the slight breeze and ran a very large circle 8 course. Nothing yielded the slightest hint of the runabout. She had simply disappeared. There were no other boats around that Hank could see and he had been glued to his binoculars for over three hours. All the while, Eva kept repeating how sorry she was.

Finally, Hank announced they had done all he knew to do so after calling Miami Coast Guard to alert them to a possible marine hazard, they resumed their course to Bimini.

After six hours they finally made it to the island where they had to observe quarantine, not leaving the boat until a Customs Officer cleared them into the country. Customs could take awhile at this hour since it was past the normal arrival time. They were tied up at the outer most dock, on the end so no one could readily see the name of the boat on the stern unless they took the time to walk all the way down the dock and leaned over the edge to catch the boats name. It was a precaution they hoped they would not need, along with registering with the dockmaster under a different name. All to avoid detection by Slayder, if he was even on the island.

Mysteriously, word had gotten out Hank was back. Bones suddenly appeared welcoming them all and gave them an update on island happenings and also inquired as to the whereabouts of the Whaler. First and foremost, the Customs Officer was on his way, his schedule accelerated by the fact he was another of Bones' cousins. Otherwise, they could have been sitting for quite some time, flying their yellow quarantine flag waiting to get cleared into Bimini. Bones did let them know there was a native tournament about to start over the next couple of days which they could enter as long as he was on board. Hank broke the news to his first mate regarding the strange disappearance of the Whaler but assured him his cousin would be reimbursed by the insurance company.

"That native tournament sounds like a plan" said Calhoun. "Given it is so late today, I think we would just like to take it easy tomorrow and start fishing on Saturday."

"I have just the thing you need to do" volunteered Bones. "My cousin has opened up a rental shop since the last time you guys were here. That is where the Whaler was headed. His name is Snowflake and he has light tackle fishing gear and a couple of small Whalers and he just got an Albury in."

"Those Albury's are nice runabouts" Hank said. "They are still made out of wood so you know how I feel about that! They are all handmade, one at a time over in Abaco at Man O' War Cay. In fact, we should run over to Abaco for a couple of days after the tournament here."

"That settles it" chimed in Eva. "Bones can you reserve the Albury through your cousin Snowflake and Calhoun and I will make a day of it tomorrow? By the way, how did he get a name like Snowflake living in the tropics?"

"You'll see tomorrow" was the only response she got as Bone's cousin, the Customs Officer, was strolling down the dock to check them in.

Chapter 26

The next day dawned cloudless and with no humidity. A perfect day to explore on a runabout. Bones came down the dock early to grab Eva so he could take her to his cousins' bait and boat rental shop. She left strict instructions with Hank to let Calhoun sleep as he was going to need his strength.

With those orders issued, she left with Bones toward the fishing village, about a twenty-minute walk. This gave her a chance to study Bones and she realized, not for the first, he was not a bad looking man. Light skinned with hazel eyes, his features seemed askew, ears that protruded, left eyebrow slightly higher than its counterpart, his nose tailed off to the right while his jaw line protruded in the opposite direction. But all the parts added up to an attractive whole.

"So, Bones, why have we not met your cousin before now?"

"He has been in Nassau for the last 5 years, only returning 2 months ago.

"And why the name, Snowflake?"

"Patience, Miss Eva."

She could tell they were approaching the fishing village by the distinctive odor of fish accompanied by the smell emanating from a mountain of empty conch shells, the remnants from the conch divers who dove for the conch meat itself, which made up the fresh conch chowder and fritters served on the island. And there was the squadron of gulls, winging around the area, looking for pieces of meat or fish wherever they could scavenge it.

This was also the location where the bonefish guides hung out in the hopes of getting a charter to fish for this elusive fighter arguably pound for pound the best fighting fish around. It's just they mostly resided in the flats and not deep water.

At the end of the dock stood a shack with the simple name Snowflakes Bait & Boat Rental hand painted across the top. And there stood a smiling Snowflake and with his sighting, Eva suddenly understood the name.

Snowflake was an Albino.

Chapter 27

"Snowflake, I want you to meet Eva. She is off the Mahalo and is the one who wants to charter your Albury for the day."

"Pleased to meet you. I will be delighted to rent you my boat…the finest on the island. Would you like some drinks and perhaps sandwiches as well?"

Eva had already anticipated that question and handed Snowflake a list of items she would need for the day.

With a quick glance he nodded his approval and summoned one of his compatriots. "Get to the grocer and get these items then go make sure the Albury is topped off and be quick. This lady has big plans for the day!"

"Let me show you the boat until my friend returns, that way you can get familiar with it. I know my cousin will show you how to run it when you leave here but my instructions need to be given as well."

"Snowflake, may I ask you a question? Are you offended by your nickname?"

"Oh, no ma'am. First, it's my real name, my mama took one look at me when I was born and called me her little snowflake. The name stuck. Not to mention there is only one Snowflake in all of the Bahamas. Everybody knows me! Long as I stay out of the sun, I'm good."

With that settled he began his crash course on how to operate the boat and was finished by the time his friend had returned with the day's provisions. Snowflake, Eva and Bones went inside to complete the paperwork while the boat was topped off with gas. Once all of that was done, Eva and Bones jumped on board the runabout, with Eva behind the wheel and Bones beside her giving directions as they made their way back to the Mahalo.

Less than five minutes later, they were pulling up alongside the Mahalo. Bones jumped onto the dive platform, carrying a bowline with him which he loosely draped around one of the cleats. He stuck his head inside the salon yelling for Mr. Hipp to let him know his ride was here.

Calhoun emerged from his stateroom inquiring as to what he needed for his adventure.

"Nothing sir. As far as I can tell Miss Eva has thought of everything. But you better get on out of here. You know how short her patience can be."

"Don't I though. Let me grab my pipe and tobacco and I'm gone. See you guys tonight. I think we are eating at Captain Browns restaurant around seven."

"That will work since Snowflake wants his boat back no later than 4:30"

"Got it." And with that he was out the door and climbing into the dingy.

Chapter 28

With Eva steering the center console Albury, they made it out of the harbor and through the jetties where she took a hard right running parallel to the island and the windward beaches. Since this area was a great deal more exposed to the elements, hardly anyone lived on this side of Bimini and the further north she went the more desolate it became.

"So, Eva, how was your meeting with Snowflake and why all the mystery with his name?"

"For one, the mystery was solved instantly as soon as I saw him. He is an Albino and thus his name. He could not have been a nicer guy. Took a great deal of time to school me on how to run this boat plus he gave me a family discount on the rental since Bones is his cousin."

"Bones is everyone's cousin on this island. I wonder if it is an honorary title or if his parent's family were the most prolific of all time!" joked Calhoun.

Eva barely heard his remark as she was focused on an underwater dark area just ahead of them. Snowflake had not mentioned anything about a reef this close to the beach and besides, it seemed to be moving but she could not be certain if the movement was just a trick her eyes were playing on her given the gentle swells from the ocean.

"Calhoun, look over there and tell me what you see" Eva said pointing to an area just off the port bow.

"I don't know, it sure is big though. Is it moving or is that a bed of coral?"

Eva took a moment before she responded. "I've been watching it and I think it's moving."

"Well given that we are about to go over the top of it, I guess we are about to find out" observed Calhoun.

Moments later they did pass over what turned out to be a massive Manta Ray. Its wingspan extended beyond either side of the boat.

"My God," exclaimed Calhoun, "Would you look at that! That thing is huge!"

"Yeah and now it's following us" said Eva.

"Speed up and try to put some distance between us."

Eva moved the throttle forward as the Albury leapt out of the water in response. She looked back to gauge how far back the ray was only to be startled to see it was keeping pace.

"Calhoun, somehow I think we pissed that thing off."

Before Calhoun had a chance to respond, he was horrified to see the giant ray leap from the water and seemingly glide toward their boat. He only had a moment to realize if that animal landed on them, they would most likely be crushed beneath it.

"LOOK OUT!" he yelled just as the ray came crashing down, a scant few feet from the racing

Albury. The Manta missed the boat but it did give everyone on board a good soaking as it landed back in the ocean.

"Good Lord, that thing just missed us!" exclaimed Calhoun.

Eva was laughing as she pushed the throttles to full open, making sure not to give the angry ray a second chance. As a result, the wind blew through her long blonde hair, whipping it in all directions.

"What in the hell is so funny?" asked Calhoun. My heartrate is through the roof!"

Eva glanced sideways back at him, mainly to keep her hair out of her face and eyes saying, "That's not the only thing gonna get your heartrate up today!"

Chapter 29

Ten minutes later she spotted a small cove-like indention in the beach, just as Snowflake had described. This area was the northern end of Bimini and was owned by a U.S. corporation which used it exclusively as a resort for their senior executives. If they were not in residence, which she was told they were not, then they had this part of the island to themselves, totally isolated with only a heavy stand of Australian Pines occupying this area. She throttled the runabout almost to a dead stop and let the incoming tide coupled with their forward momentum carry them onto the beach. "Calhoun, jump out and carry the anchor line with you so you can plant the anchor further up on the beach."

"Yes ma'am!" came the sarcastic response.

It took only a moment to secure the anchor and pull the boat further ashore.

"Now, may I ask what you are up to?" queried Calhoun

"After you get the picnic basket, cooler and blankets out and put them in the shade of those pine trees."

Once that was done, Calhoun looked back at Eva with his hands extended, palms up. "Well?"

"Calhoun, have you never had a beach picnic?"

"Not really."

"Have you ever made love on the beach?"

It never failed how her frankness surprised him. It had been like that since day one and these scant years later it still caught him off guard.

"A couple of years ago in the surf at Honeymoon Beach"

"Nope! Doesn't count. That was in the surf, I said on the beach."

"Well then the answer is no."

"I didn't think so. We are going to change that right now."

"Here? Now?" asked a clearly nervous Calhoun as he looked around only to realize they were totally alone without a soul or boat or dwelling for that matter in sight.

Eva had already unrolled the blanket. She sat down and patted the area next to her. "Come here Calhoun. Let's make a memory."

And what a memory it was!

Later, as they lay on the beach drinking wine in the nude, Eva asked "Have you ever had a nude lunch before?"

"Nope!"

"Well then look at all the firsts we have achieved on our first full day back! Just imagine what we might accomplish with 3 weeks!" Calhoun missed the twinkle in Eva's eye for he had already drifted off.

It wasn't long before the combination of food, wine, sun and physical exertion had her sleepy as well. It only took another moment for them both to be asleep, intwined in each other's arms with just a blanket as a covering.

A shadow passed over her. At least she thought so. Could have been a dream but what was that tickling her foot? Was it Calhoun being playful? Or a crab being exploratory? Whichever it was, she did not want to wake up to see. She was in that realm between sleep and wakefulness and right now she chose sleep.

There it was again, a slight nudge on her foot. Now she was awake and none too happy about it. She was not sure how long she had been asleep but she knew she was not ready to wake up. She leaned up bracing on one arm, shaded her eyes with her free hand and decided to open them. She immediately regretted that decision.

Before her stood Slayder. Eva's shock was so complete she could only utter one word while flailing with her free hand the area Calhoun had previously occupied.

"How?"

"Don't you worry about how and you can stop trying to feel around to find your lover. He was gone when I got here. Now here's the deal. Those bales of marijuana you had confiscated cost me a million and a half dollars and I want that money back and want it quick so I can replace it. There is a music festival about to take place in upstate New York and I need that inventory to sell there. Understood?"

Eva nodded in the affirmative.

"You have ten days. I'll be back then. And by the way," giving her a long, appraising look over, "you are looking mighty fine."

Eva clutched the blanket against her, feeling as though she had just been violated, as she watched Slayder disappear into the grove of pine trees.

Chapter 30

She sat there, knees pulled to her chest, shivering. It had all happened so fast she began to wonder if she had imagined the whole thing. But no, it was real enough.

It was then Calhoun came bounding over the dune behind her, "Hey Eva, I saw some tire tracks over …"

He stopped suddenly as he realized something was wrong. "Eva?"

He ran the balance of the way, dropping to his knees and grabbing her around the shoulders in an awkward hug. "What's happened?"

"Slayder. He's back." And with that she broke down into long, deep sobs as she recounted what had just occurred.

Once Calhoun ascertained Eva was not physically injured, he helped to get her dressed and back to the boat. She sat next to him, glassy eyed, as he raced back toward the harbor and the relative safety of the Mahalo.

They were all gathered in the bar area of the Compleat Angler as it was not yet open for the day and Bowers had graciously offered it to the group. Hank, Bones, Eva, Calhoun and the local police. Once Calhoun had gotten back to the Mahalo, Hank took charge, arranging for the meeting to discuss next steps while Bones returned the Albury to his cousin.

Eva was recovered enough to give a coherent account of what had taken place although her story did not waiver from her initial recollection as shared with Calhoun. Without question, the Mahalo would be placed under local police protection. A call from the wireless shack had resulted in the U.S. Marshalls committing to flying in two agents. No one had any idea as to how Slayder got on the island, much less how he had managed to track Eva down. And how had he managed to get his hands on a car where there were so few private cars on the island as most people walked, rode bicycles or motor scooters? The price of petrol and import fees alone kept the inventory of cars in check. Nevertheless, they knew they had to have a strategy moving forward. The first leg was to make sure Calhoun could come up with the money if all else failed. He would make the necessary calls after an early dinner. The second leg was to have the Mahalo fish the local tournament they had already committed to, with a shadow boat also fishing but with the two Marshalls acting as fishermen and staying in close proximity in case Slayder was foolish enough to make another appearance. Additionally, another of Bones cousins, Shoestring, would come on board the Mahalo as an extra mate. In the meantime, the police would canvas all the car owners to determine where their vehicles had been today.

With that settled, they left the Compleat Angler to go up the street to Captain Browns Restaurant where they partook in a subdued meal of fresh kingfish with the requisite island side dishes. Tomorrow would bring the tournament and perhaps a chance to finally capture their nemesis.

Chapter 31

The morning was cloudless but with a northeast wind blowing steady and hard enough to have the seas running between 3-4 feet. A nice chop, thought Hank. Just enough wave action to bring the billfish to the surface in hunt for food. Bones and Shoestring were already on board, baits were made up and ready but Hank remained tied up at the dock as he had not seen Calhoun or Eva and he wanted them to get as much sleep as possible. He figured another 10 minutes then he would crank up the engines and start heading out toward the tournament boat. As he sat up on the flying bridge, he heard a horn sound as the Albury Eva had rented the day before passed by with a captain and two anglers who were both dressed in long kakis and long sleeved starched white shirts. They could not have advertised any clearer they were feds. So much for undercover thought Hank. But they did look as though they were fully rigged for a day of fishing so he hoped they could perhaps enjoy their overwatch and catch a few fish.

He had no sooner entertained that thought then Eva stuck her head up peering onto the bridge while standing halfway up on the ladder. "Morning Hank."

"Good Morning Eva. Sleep alright? You guys ok?"

"I needed that rest. Makes yesterday feel unreal but Calhoun and I talked last night and we are not going to let yesterday's encounter ruin our trip. We both agree we need to carry on as planned."

"Good to hear" replied Hank as he turned the ignitions to both engines to get them started. "Bones, Shoestring, get those dock lines off and let's go win us a tournament!"

The airhorn resonated through the radio indicating time for the boats to get going on their shotgun start. Hank had been watching some birds working just to the north and pushed his throttles full forward to get there as quickly as possible. As far as he could tell, there were about 20-25 boats fishing the tournament. He liked his odds.

As he raced to the spot where he wanted to drop his lines, Eva and Calhoun sat in the fighting chairs talking amongst themselves.

"Calhoun, I know I have told you this before, but you lucked up when you found Hank."

"I know. It was just great timing as he was available at the exact time I was looking. Been three years now and I wouldn't change a thing. He is a great skipper, mechanic, cook and guide. I like our chances with him behind the wheel. He knows it all."

The run out to the area Hank had identified as to where he wanted to start trolling had a cathartic effort. The steady hum of the diesels accompanied with the gentle roll of the boat caused by the following seas had Eva practically hypnotized.

Hank looked behind him and spotted the Albury far back but following. He turned around and kept his eyes on the solitary bird swooping low and occasionally diving into the ocean for bait fish. It was a Man of War and where those birds worked for food, larger fish were sure to be nearby. He smiled to himself as he felt this was a good omen.

Twenty minutes later Hank throttled back to trolling speed and yelled down to get the lines out. With two mates, this task took no time and as a result, Hank began his figure 8 trolling pattern while other skippers were trying to get to the spots where they wanted to start their day. As far as Hank was concerned, advantage – Mahalo!

"ONE! ONE!" came the cry from the bridge as Calhoun's line was spit from the outrigger clip and his rod began a slight bow. It had been less than five minutes and they had their first fish on the line. Calhoun quickly placed the rod from the holder to the gimbal and began reeling. "Whatever it is," he yelled, "it's not big."

"Keep reeling!" came the command from Hank who was in his element right now and would not tolerate anything less than a fully focused fishing team.

Shoestring stood behind Calhoun's chair and as the leader wire came up, he grabbed it and pulled into the cockpit a most unusual looking fish.

Hank raced down the ladder ordering Bones topside to continue to follow the Man of War. He took a look at the fish and shook his head before putting it onto the ice in the fish box.

"Hank, what is that?" asked Calhoun. Hank mumbled a reply, got the line replenished with a new bait, ran it up the outrigger, then turned and raced through the salon and into the crew's quarters.

"What was that thing?" he said to himself as he reached under his mattress and pulled out a fishing book and began to look up just what they had on board. A few moments later he came up into the cockpit where Calhoun repeated his earlier question.

"Why, that's a Cobia, Mr. Hipp." And with that Hank continued to explain how big they got, how good they were to eat and how to cook them. With a smile on his face he ascended the ladder to his perch, replacing Bones, fully satisfied with himself. "Yep," he thought. "This is going to be a good day."

Below, in the cockpit, Calhoun leaned over to Eva's ear and whispered, "See Honey, I told you he was the best. He knows everything!"

Chapter 32

It appeared the Cobia may have been the highlight of their day as they went through the balance of the morning with nothing more than two barracuda to show for it. They had long chased off the Man of War as he apparently got weary of being followed around. Listening on the radio, Hank could monitor what other boats were doing. A couple of sails, some dolphin, wahoo and kingfish with a smattering of barracuda was all the entire tournament had to show for their morning efforts. Hank could only be thankful for the fact they were still in competition. No one was pulling away. The shadow boat was about 300 yards away and Hank could only feel sorry for them as they had no shelter from the sun or heat. The long sleeve shirts and pants suddenly made sense as the Marshalls would be burned up without them.

Lunch time came and they all went down to the galley one at a time to make their sandwiches. Hank was a serious tournament competitor and he wanted most of his crew at or near their designated area. Both Eva and Calhoun ate standing up, just inside the salon doors where they could enjoy a brief respite from the heat in the confines of the air conditioning, but be near enough to grab their lines if anything hit. Morning bled into early afternoon.

Inaction, heat and sun can make the most disciplined crew lethargic and the Mahalo group was no exception. Bones and Shoestring alternated going up to the bridge to help keep Hank sharp and to add another set of eyes to follow the trailing baits. Occasionally one of them would come down and snap a line out of the rigger and reel the bait in to make sure they were good and not nipped by a barracuda. The minutes crawled by.

Bones was up top with Hank when suddenly the number two bait was crashed. "TWO! TWO!" yelled out Hank and Bones simultaneously. Shoestring moved with catlike reflexes and had the rod in Calhoun's hands almost instantly. Hank throttled back to a dead slow and then handed the boat off to Bones, "You know what to do. Keep our stern to that fish!" Bones nodded his head in confirmation. Hank was immediately in the cockpit assisting Shoestring with clearing the other three lines and actually put the rods inside the salon acknowledging this would be the last fish they planned on fighting for the day.

"Okay everyone, we are hooked into a big blue marlin. I need everyone to play their part. Shoestring, you stand behind Mr. Hipp and keep his chair angled toward that fish. Eva, you keep him hydrated with water and even throw a bucket of seawater on him to keep him cool if need be. Mr. Hipp, keep that line tight. You know he will make a couple of runs at us. Do not lose this fish! This could be THE tournament fish. Everyone understand?" Nods all around. Hank went back up topside, switching places with Bones. Hank glanced at his watch; it was 2PM straight up. He radioed the tournament boat to inform them the Mahalo was hooked up with a blue.

For the next thirty minutes, the battle between fish and angler went on with a fury. The marlin made a couple of leaps but Calhoun kept the line taunt by reeling in fast when given those opportunities. Hank kept the marlin dead astern. Everyone was focused and doing their job when suddenly the sound of a gunshot resonated throughout the cockpit.

Chapter 33

Eva screamed and everyone else, including Calhoun, instinctively ducked. Bones was the first to recover his wits. There was no gunshot, it was the pop of the rod breaking just above the reel seat. The sound had been amplified by the tight quarters of the cockpit.

"Hank, the damn rod has broken!" yelled Bones.

"How about the line?" asked Hank. But before Bones could respond the answer came from the marlin as he made another leap trying to shake the hook. "Bones, get back up here. I need to be in the cockpit."

As soon as he returned to the cockpit, Hank asked if everyone was okay. Startled and pissed off by this sudden change of fortune were the responses he got.

"Mr. Hipp, keep reeling but do not let the line hit the broken part of the rod or it will break the line and we will lose this fish." Hank then showed Calhoun how to guide the line away from any ragged edges.

"Shoestring, hold the broken rod, I have some surgery to perform" With that Hank removed the screws from the roller guides of the broken rod and did the same from a twin rod of the disabled one. He then put the new rod into the reel seat, and put the line into the new blank and finished up by replacing the screws into the roller guide. It was a total team effort which took less than 10 minutes. Hank congratulated everyone, especially Calhoun for keeping the marlin on and for keeping the line from breaking. "Now reel, Mr. Hipp! Recess is over." smiled Hank as he went back to the bridge. He could hear over the radio several boats chattering that the Mahalo had a big fish on. "You guys have no way of knowing the drama we just had in the cockpit" Hank thought.

Thirty minutes later, Hank could tell the fish was tiring. Calhoun was gaining more line than was going out. The captain was encouraged the battle was nearing an end. Then suddenly the same sickening sound they had heard earlier, came again. The second rod had broken in the same place as the first!

The only thing left to do was to tighten the drag on the reel and bring the marlin into the boat where Shoestring and Bones gaffed and boated the fish. Shoestring had tears in his eyes and Bones was cussing for all he was worth as Hank radioed into the tournament boat the Mahalo had boated the marlin but was disqualifying the catch. Once an angler is helped by other people to bring in a fish, that fish must be disqualified. They had battled this big blue for just shy of two hours. When Hank replaced the radio microphone back in its clip, he looked around to see several boats, including the Albury, with their crews standing and applauding the Mahalo.

When the Mahalo, with its demoralized crew, returned to the weigh in dock they put the marlin up and found it came in at 445 pounds. It led the day and ultimately would have won the tournament as the largest fish taken. The Cobia, which was eaten that night, came in at 4 pounds. It was the only Cobia caught in those waters for the balance of the season. Hemingway would have been proud.

The day ended with a totally exhausted crew and without a single thought of Slayder.

Chapter 34

The final day of the tournament dawned as a mirror image of the day before, the only difference on the Mahalo was the fact Shoestring was not going to be able to mate as he was active in his church and could not miss a day of worship. No one was going to argue that point. Hank was up top when the Albury came alongside. While the captain held his boat in place, one of the Marshalls jumped aboard the Mahalo which caused both Eva and Calhoun to come out of the salon where they had been enjoying their morning coffee. Calhoun was dressed in his "good luck" fishing shorts while she had on her usual bikini but this time, she was wearing her top.

At the sight of Eva, the boarder puffed out his chest and introduced himself. "Good Morning folks. I'm Harris Chewning with the U.S. Marshalls Service, which I think you may have figured out. Nice catch yesterday, quite a battle only surpassed by the integrity you showed when you disqualified that fish. Most impressive. Anyway, I did not come here to discuss that. We believe we have found out how Slayder got on the island a couple of days ago. U.S. Coast Guard reports there is a Cuban fishing trawler just over the horizon but well within international waters. A couple of flyovers by their helicopter says their nets are out as though they are trolling for shrimp. The name on the stern is the Revolucion. I know that is the same boat you guys had a hand in busting awhile back. Our guess is Slayder is on that boat and had it bring him in closer to shore under cover of darkness where he waited to make his move. I also understand no one has admitted to letting him use their car but as you know most people just leave their keys in the ignition around here. After all, where would you go? We are going to follow you again today although we are certain nothing will take place. By the way, shadowing you guys was good luck for us, we got four dolphin that we plan on taking the filets home tonight. Any questions?"

Hearing none, Marshall Chewning gave a boy scout two finger salute and reboarded the Albury so they could head out to sea.

"Well, now, that was interesting" observed Eva.

"Told us a whole lot of nothing, typical government speak" groused Calhoun. "Seems to me the type of guy who got pushed down in the mud puddle during his high school years. But now he has the badge. By the way Eva, what's with the top? You've' been topless for so long that its almost sexier when you are dressed!"

"If you must know, the twins were getting a bit too much sun so I've decided to cover them for a while!"

"If you guys are through yakking, let's get this show on the road. We aren't out of this yet!" said Hank as he instructed Bones and Calhoun the order of which lines to get off so they could join the tournament.

Chapter 35

The day stayed extremely hot which meant most of the billfish remained lower in the ocean where the cooler waters flowed. Morning turned to afternoon with only one small dolphin and two barracuda to show for it. Three o'clock came as the spirits on the Mahalo lagged. One thing about sport fishing, it is often long tedious hours followed by moments of frenzied activity. It was the nature of the sport.

ZIPZING followed by "FOUR, FOUR" from the flybridge. Eva's line. It was Bones who had done the yelling as he was on the bridge as part of the rotation, he and Hank went through in order to stay alert. They would both move between the cockpit and the bridge about every hour. Hank grabbed the rod out of the side holder and gave it to Eva. "Billfish!" Yelled a jubilant Bones.

This would be the first billfish of the tournament for Eva which may be the first for a female angler during the tournament. "Okay Calhoun, I'm bringing this bitch home!" She smiled her famous dimple smile as her green eyes lit up with determination. She was focused. And it was a good thing too as she had a fighter on the line, one that was mad and would take out line then rush the boat. Hank stayed behind her, swiveling her seat as necessary to keep the proper angle on the quarry while gently coaching her all the while. In the meantime, Calhoun got busy bringing in the other lines and stowing them away in the main salon.

Everyone was busy for the first fifteen minutes which only aggravated Hank when he heard another captain call into the tournament boat over the radio that the Mahalo was hooked up but hadn't reported the hook up. Hank, who was still steamed over yesterday, ran into the main salon where the second radio was located and snarled into the microphone that he was pretty busy right now. With that, he was back into the cockpit where he could manage the fish. Once he was satisfied Eva had control, he went back and called the tournament boat to report that the Mahalo did indeed have a billfish on.

Eva continued her battle for another 45 minutes before she brought alongside a nice sailfish. Hank gaffed it and got it on board. As it turned out, the sail weighed in at 124 pounds which, along with the other fish she had caught previously, got Eva the top female angler award. While the Mahalo did not win the tournament outright, they did win the Calcutta totaling over $20,000. Calhoun insisted those monies be split between the crew as Hank saw fit. Once again, not a single thought about Slayder for the entire day. Hank did notice the Marshalls did not attend the awards ceremony leading him to believe they may have already left the island with their coolers full of dolphin filets.

The awards evening was held back at the Calypso Club where the spirits flowed freely and the native food was served up in abundance. In other words, everyone indulged, perhaps too much. The crew of the Mahalo staggered home from the festivities, singing about what your daddy didn't know, in every key imaginable. With arms interlaced, they could just have well been on the yellow brick road skipping their way to see the mighty wizard. Their attention thus occupied; they did not notice the two shadow figures following them along on the other side of the street.

Upon their return to the boat, Eva insisted on "just one more." Calhoun grabbed a Johnny Walker and water along with two rum and cokes with limes for Eva and Hank then made his way to the cockpit where they could enjoy the evenings air and rehash the day. Hank had turned on the underwater stern lights illuminating the area below. This was always interesting as one never knew what sea life may come floating or swimming by. As it turned out, this evening would be no different. After about five minutes of being on, something jumped from the water and hit Eva in the leg causing her to let out a startled yelp. Then another and another. Calhoun leaned over the transom and was shocked to see an entire school of shrimp, so many they appeared as a white cloud beneath the lights of the Mahalo.

"They are attracted to the lights" Hank said. "Let's stand back and see if we can let enough jump on board to cook up later." Eventually, to everyone's surprise, they ended up with just a few shrimp shy of forty. "Lunch tomorrow with my 'World Famous BBQ Shrimp'."

"A most interesting day" observed Eva as they gathered up the shrimp, finished their drinks and turned in but not before killing the underwater stern lights.

Chapter 36

As the tournament was over, there was no timetable to adhere to. Thus Hank "allowed" Eva and Calhoun to sleep in until 7:30 at which point he decided it was time to get moving. Standing outside of their stateroom door, he held the biggest pot and the heaviest ladle the Mahalo had and started banging on the pot for all he was worth. Loud, but effective as he could tell from the yells to please stop that he had accomplished his goal.

"Engines will crank up in fifteen minutes. We have some fishing to do so let's move it!"

Eva turned to Calhoun as she gingerly slipped out of bed; "I thought drill sergeants were just in the Army. Did they have them in the Navy too?"

"Apparently," came the muttered response.

To ease the pain exacerbated by the glaring sun, Hank decided to play some soothing music to give his anglers a bit of headache relief. He popped a selection into the eight-track player where instantly the music of Sergio Mendes and Brasil 66 filled the cabin as well as the cockpit. Eva had claimed her customary seat and sipped on a Bloody Mary in hopes it would alleviate the pounding reminder from the previous evenings indulgence of Planters Punches. Calhoun elected to stay in the air conditioning of the main salon but close enough to the doors that he could be in his seat in a matter of seconds.

"Feeling a little rough, are we?" teased Hank as he put the rod rigged with a wire line in the holder on her chair. "This should make you feel better."

Eva had seen the wireline before and had actually caught a good-sized Snapper on one sometime back. Wire lines are more like bottom lines as opposed to the surface lines of monofilament more commonly used. This line was made of wire and designed to plumb the depths two to three hundred feet below the boat. She also knew from experience these lines were challenges to reel in even without a fish on due to the weights it carried necessary to get the bait to sink to the desired depth. These lines did not go up in the outriggers but trailed directly behind and below the boat. Thus, one had to be alert as to when a fish was on. If the wire did not start running off the reel, the only other sign would be the sudden bent in the rod.

"Eva, pay attention. Keep your fingers lightly on the wire so you will know if you have anything on. Lightly is key unless you want to have this line deep burn you on its way out!"

"Understood"

They were trolling back in the direction of Honeymoon Beach. There were three other surface lines out but Hank was banking on the wire line to provide the action once they cleared the Bimini Shelf and hit some deeper water.

The sun beat down without mercy. Eva managed to sweat out the balance of her alcohol and as a result she became drowsy. The music lulled her into a deep sleep but with her fingers lightly caressing the wire line.

Hank had hoped for this moment. He motioned to Bones to come topside and take over the bridge while he scampered quietly back to the cockpit. He gingerly pulled in the line holding the bait closest to Eva and switched it out with a five gallon wash bucket. Stealth being the key, Hank lowered the bucket into the water, snapped the line back into the rigger and bolted up to the bridge. Within seconds water filled the bucket causing it to snap out of the rigger to a sound everyone knew.

"ONE! ONE!" yelled Hank. "Eva, grab that rod and get busy! Nap time is over!"

The weight of the water - filled bucket being pulled at trolling speed caused the rod to bend almost forty-five degrees.

"Hank, I need help. This must be a huge fish. Did you see it?"

"Too many questions! Get that rod in the chair and get busy. Keep that line tight!"

Eva managed to wrestle the rod into the holder between her legs and for the next ten minutes she fought with her unknown adversary. Little did she know Hank was controlling the fight. If he wanted Eva to be able to reel line in, he kept the boat in neutral. If the "fish" made a run, it did so only because Hank had put the boat in forward, thus increasing the drag on the line. By now Calhoun was in the cockpit, curious as to what Eva may have on. When he called up to Hank to inquire, he got a one word response, "Bucketfish."

The joke had run its course, especially since the boss was now involved. Hank put the boat in neutral and told Eva the fish was tired and to reel hard. Hank descended the steps from the flying bridge to the cockpit and stood in the corner nearest to Eva ready to grab the wire lead once it came up.

"Bucketfish? Why have we never caught one before? Are they good to eat? How big do they get?" Eva was an endless series of questions.

"Hang on. You are about to see for yourself." And with that Hank leaned over the transom and pulled the bucket up and over in one quick and fluid motion, spilling the water and intentionally soaking Eva in the process.

Chapter 37

Eva's look of surprise was so fleeting, Hank later wondered if it had actually happened. She had been taken off guard again. After the potato and sinking joke, she swore she would never let Hank get the better of her a second time. Well he had, kudos to him but don't let him know it. Rather than scream, which is what she so desperately wanted to do, she let out a big "AHHHH." The water did feel good against the heat of the day, it was the delivery of it that got her. "Thanks, Hank. I needed that."

Calhoun was grinning from ear to ear but one quick sideways glance from Eva wiped it clean off his face. Hank may get the jump on her but Calhoun did not have to enjoy it so much. She would deal with him later. Bones let out a quick laugh from his observation post on the bridge, shook his head and returned to the Captain's chair. Hank, was clearly disappointed his antics hadn't gotten a bigger reaction. She was one tough cookie and keeping her cool the way she did only improved her standing with the Captain.

"So much for my world famous Bucketfish joke. At least you are fully awake now so let's concentrate on the wireline and see what we can really catch! Bones, steer toward Honeymoon Beach. We should be at a good depth for the wireline in about ten minutes."

"Got it" said the affable first mate.

They had just cleared the shallows and were off the Bimini Shelf when the wire line got first one, then two quick tugs before the line went screaming off the reel. This time they were hooked onto something more substantial than a bucket. Hank was still in the cockpit so he yelled up to Bones to put the boat in neutral as he assisted Eva in getting the rod secured in the gimble between her legs. Once situated, Eva braced herself by putting her feet up on the fish box directly in front of her and lowering the rod, reeling hard as she did and pulling back with both hands only to repeat the process.

"Any ideas what we could have?" she asked.

"No clue, but let's concentrate on getting it on board." Hank replied.

Another ten minutes passed with Eva slowly winning the battle as she added more line than went out. Hank had positioned himself at the same place he had been earlier but this time with a gaff in hand.

"Keep coming Eva and when I say 'all the way back', I want you to pull the rod as far back as you can."

Before she could respond, Hank leaned all the way over, grabbed the line and yelled "ALL THE WAY BACK." Eva complied as Hank reached with the gaff and hooked the fish. "Grouper," he reported and swung the fish on board and into the fish box slamming the lid on top.

"Looks to be about eight pounds or so" he observed.

"Gosh, that thing sure felt like it weighed a lot more than that!" Eva said in astonishment.

"The thing about groupers is they come up with their mouths wide open so you are pulling against all that water too, which makes it feel heavier than it actually is. Good news is we have dinner! Bones, take us to Honeymoon."

Chapter 38

Thirty minutes later they had dropped anchor in the same inlet they had seen so much action in. Hank got busy prepping the 'catch' from last night in his self-proclaimed "World Famous BBQ Shrimp" as he so repeatedly reminded them. Since this meal was messy and required an oven, they stayed on the Mahalo for lunch. While the meal was cooking, Eva and Calhoun decided to snorkel in the vicinity of the Mahalo. All it would take is a quick airhorn blast to signal the two to come in for lunch. There were two other day boats at anchor in the inlet, their passengers no doubt seeking a respite from the boiling midday sun since neither appeared to be rigged for off shore fishing.

Calhoun and Eva were swimming along, holding hands and observing the sea life as it unfolded below them. It was easy to get hypnotized by this other world and lose sense of anything else around you and that is why Calhoun was startled when Eva suddenly clamped down on his arm with both hands and tried to come to an abrupt stop but their forward momentum continued to carry them a few more yards. Eva started to frantically back pedal as she pointed to something on the ocean floor just ahead of them that they were about to pass over. Calhoun tried to follow her gestures as she pulled hard on his arm in an effort to get him to reverse course. He looked at her and saw the obvious panic in her eyes, then looked again at the form taking shape now beneath them. SHARK! It was just lying on the sandy bottom below them. Its skin nearly matched the color of the ocean floor thus the reason they did not see it any earlier. He did not need any convincing to join Eva in beating a hasty retreat but something told him not to make any sudden or panicked moves. Eva headed back toward the Mahalo as Calhoun back peddled keeping a wary eye on the shark below. Suddenly, with a forceful whip of its tail, the animal shot out from its resting place and turned toward the two snorkelers. Almost simultaneously, the airhorn on the Mahalo sounded in three short blasts followed by three longer ones and ending in three short blasts. His combat experience paid off as Calhoun recognized the universal sequence for SOS.

"Tell me something I don't know." He thought. No need trying to outrace this guy so all he could do was to keep back peddling and keep the shark in sight. He risked a quick glance ahead and saw Eva was almost to the Mahalo. He knew he was giving off whatever panic vibes a shark could sense so he nearly jumped out of the water when the Mahalo's engines started and she moved forward. The result was a virtual sandstorm as the prop wash from the boat kicked up a cloud of sand off the bottom obscuring everything. "Damnit to hell. What are those guys doing?" Now he had lost sight of the shark.

There was no need to continue to look for the shark since he could not see anything beyond five feet anyway. He decided to swim as hard as he could in the direction of the Mahalo where he last saw it. He did not want to break any rhythm in his swimming so he kept his head down, breathed through his snorkel, and freestyled his way as quickly as he was able. Within seconds, which felt like years, he bumped into the stern area of his boat where two sets of hands grabbed and lifted him onto the stern swim platform. He tucked his legs underneath him, looking up at Bones and Hank who had jerked him onboard, just as a dorsal fin glided by and headed out to open sea.

"Lemon shark" said Hank. "Probably would not have hurt you, but you never know."

Eva leaned over the transom and gave Calhoun a huge hug proclaiming him as her hero in a teasing falsetto voice.

As soon as Calhoun could gather his wits he lashed out at his crew.

"What the hell were you guys thinking starting the engines and blinding me in the sandstorm it kicked up?"

Bones took full responsibility. "As soon as I saw the shark, I sounded the SOS to let you know. It seemed to me to be coming right at you so I thought the sound of the engines would scare it off. The sandstorm was just an added benefit."

The look on Bones' face was so pitiful, Calhoun could not stay angry as he knew his first mate only had his well being in mind. After a couple of deep breaths, Calhoun looked Bones in the eye saying, "Thanks, Bones. You may have saved my life."

Before things got to sappy, Hank stood up from the platform and announced lunch would be ready in five minutes.

“This is fabulous!” crowed Eva as she smacked at the shrimp while simultaneously licking her fingers. “A little messy but fabulous.”

“Don’t forget to use some of that Bimini bread to sop it up with” suggested Hank.

They all were indulging in the shrimp feast before them so everyone was startled when they heard a knocking on the starboard side of the boat.

“What the hell?” exclaimed Hank as he got up to see what or who that was. He opened the salon doors, walked onto the cockpit, and peered over the side. He was stunned by what greeted him.

“Hello Captain. Permission to come aboard?”

With little recourse as he saw it, Hank told the three men sitting in the dingy to come on up.

U.S. Marshall Harris Chewning smiled as he and his fellow Marshalls tied their dingy to a cleat and scampered aboard.

Chapter 39

Hank knew he had been stunned by this unexpected arrival but he could not wait to see the looks on the faces of the other three. He slid open the salon door and announced "Mr. Hipp, Eva, I believe you know these guys." Then he stood aside as the three Marshalls crossed over the threshold into the main salon. Hank was not disappointed as everyone inside stopped in mid bite as their respective jaws dropped.

Calhoun was the first to recover his wits. "What the hell are you guys doing out here? Where did you come from? How did you find us? I thought you were gone once the tournament was over."

"Good. That's what we wanted everyone to think. Mind if we sit while you finish lunch, which by the way, smells delicious?"

"Suddenly, I think I'm full" replied Calhoun.

The others followed suit so with lunch out of the way, Harris introduced his fellow Marshalls.

"We are in those two boats anchored over there. We took a chance you guys might take a break here. We know how much you love this beach." As he spoke that last line, he looked directly at Eva which caused her to blush thinking she and Calhoun may have been observed. "We have kept a loose tail on you to make sure you come to no harm. In that process we picked up another tail on you. Two guys, neither of which is Slayder or we would have grabbed him. So, it seems every time you guys venture out into Alice Town, there is a virtual parade of people following you right along."

Chewning's last remark hung in the air while everyone on board considered its ramifications. Not sure what to say next, Calhoun spoke up.

"Well you look more local than you did last time we saw you."

And they all three did look more relaxed in their fishing shorts, tee-shirts and sandals. And they all had tans.

"Anyway," Chewning continued, "we are here to talk about Slayder. As you know, he has a rather large drug smuggling ring in this area. You stumbled across part of that sometime back. We know he wants restitution but we believe he wants more. There's this big concert in upstate New York with a whole bunch of hippies coming to it in a couple of weeks. Our intel tells us he not only wants to push the marijuana he has but that he is now branching out into cocaine and maybe heroin. We need to stop him, catch him and incarcerate him and you guys, we hope, will assist us in that endeavor. That's why there are three of us now so we can maintain twenty-four-hour surveillance on you."

Eva let out a long sigh. "You just said a mouthful without saying anything. We just want to be rid of him so we can lead our lives. You had him once in custody, how do we know you can keep him captured if you do grab him? And what is the fixation he has with me? I guess, most importantly, how do we fit in?"

"Eva, first, I cannot begin to understand the criminal mind. We have a whole army of shrinks who study their behavior. From that certain patterns emerge.

Apparently, he fantasizes his relationship with you is more than it actually is.

As far as fitting in, I'm afraid it's not a 'we' as much as it is a 'you,'" Chewning replied.

Chapter 40

"OH, HELL NO!" shouted Calhoun as he rapidly advanced to a tirade state. "They are not using Eva as bait in some hare-brained scheme to draw Slayder out. Hell, they aren't even positive if he is around."

Chewning and the other two officers had departed after sharing a plan they believed might lead to Slayder's capture.

Eva tried to soothe Calhoun as best she could. "But if he is here, it just might work. Look, Calhoun, the worst decision I ever made was coming here with that guy. And the best decision I ever made was coming here with that guy as it led me to you. Now I need to see what, if anything, I can do to put him behind bars so we can start living our lives without fear of his being around every corner. I want my life back...no wait, I want OUR lives back and if using me accomplishes that, then we win. We are lucky this New York concert has advanced his timetable to get his hands on drugs he and his folks can deal. He does not want to miss a potentially big payday."

"I don't care," retorted Calhoun. "This could potentially be your life we are talking about. What's the big deal about some New York concert anyway?"

"I've looked at the bands they have booked. It would be so cool to be able to hear them. Anybody who's anybody will be there. I don't know what could be near there as I've never heard of Woodstock, New York."

"And I bet you never will again" predicted Calhoun.

"Hey, let's get back on track here" interjected Hank. "Are you going through with this Eva"

"Yeah, I think so." I would just like to pull the Band-Aid off and get this over."

"Well, you won't be alone." stated Bones. "You see, I have these…"

"Cousins" interrupted Eva with a smile.

"Yeah and they will be out tonight. You may not notice them but they will be watching out for you"

"Thank you Bones. You're very sweet. I feel better already."

"One last thing Eva," said a much concerned Calhoun. "Keep the alcohol down if not out altogether. I want you to have your wits about you when you are walking back and forth from the Anchors Aweigh tonight."

With less than two strides to cross the salon, Eva reached out and cupped Calhoun's face in both her hands.

"You are such a sweet, sweet man" she cooed. "I will be fine" as she kissed him squarely on the mouth. She pulled back. Looked at him with those green eyes. Whenever she examined him this way, he always nearly collapsed as he felt she could really see straight into his very essence. "Now, why don't you come below and help me pick out what I'm wearing tonight. I've been thinking about the dress you bought me back in Greenville at your aunt's store."

"Halfacre-Osborne?"

"Yep. That one. Who would have thought you could find a Peter Max designed dress there? I love the psychedelic neon paisley design. It is a perfect summer dress."

"I would agree. I love the way it clings to you in all the right places!"

With a playful slap Eva pulled away and looked over her shoulder as she descended the steps to their stateroom. "Why don't you help me try it on?"

"Yes, why don't I?"

As the couple disappeared below, Hank cranked the engines to return them to Bimini and what lay ahead.

Chapter 41

The shower in the master stateroom is barely large enough for one person so it goes without saying two people are a really tight squeeze. It mattered not as Eva insisted Calhoun join her. There were no complaints with him as he found the full body contact dictated by the tight quarters very arousing. It wasn't long before Hank figured out what sort of acrobatics were going on below so he took care of the situation by cutting the breakers to the shower and master stateroom plunging the occupants into twilight and with no water to rinse off as well. It took about five minutes of pleading from Eva for Hank to restore the water before he acquiesced. However, he conveniently forgot to flip on the switch for hot water, leaving both occupants an unwanted chance to cool down. If, nothing else, his antics proved to once again to be a tension breaker.

Forty minutes later Eva emerged from the stateroom in the Peter Max mini-skirt. Hank had to agree that it did cling to her in all the right ways.

"I feel like I should have a drink because I damn sure need one."

"Careful there." Said Hank. "Keep your wits about you and your head on a swivel. From what I understand, you'll have plenty of 'cousins' watching over you.

Calhoun came up the stairs pausing on the upper most tread. “I sure wish I could go with you but I understand the fact Slayder may have someone watching the boat so get out of here before I change my mind. By the way, you look ravenous!”

“Thanks. I love you too.” Before he could respond, Eva had spun on her flats and sailed out the salon door to whatever destiny lay in wait.

Chapter 42

The Anchors Aweigh was just a bit on the other side of the Compleat Angler, giving her time to become accustomed to her surroundings. The inn itself resembled more of a plantation style home, a noticeable departure from the stucco buildings adorned with various pastel colors found elsewhere in Alice Town. Inside, was one central dining area which could accommodate twenty or so people at any given time. This evening there seemed to be a lot of people outside milling around as she slowly walked down the main street in Alice Town. This made Eva wonder how many were 'cousins'. The thought caused her to smile. She trudged up the earthen road, head down but her eyes were darting everywhere. As she came to her destination, she breathed a sigh of relief. There, on the corner, stood Snowflake, holding court with several other men. He gave her an almost imperceptible nod as she turned off the road and into the restaurant. So far, so good. And what a stroke of genius on Bones behalf she thought. Posting someone as noticeable as Snowflake would almost certainly be discounted by Slayder if he thought she was being watched.

The evening was a private dinner hosted by a German hotel manager from Paradise Island and his beautiful girlfriend. She was the head chef at the same hotel and they had made it to Bimini to fish and relax before the Marshalls Service enlisted their assistance with this well publicized invitation only event even if it was closed to the public. The purported reason for the dinner was to try several new recipes before they brought them back to Paradise Island.

As it happened, Eva was damn happy she did not have a drink before she left the boat as every course, from appetizers to dessert was liberally laced with rum. By the time the meal was over, her head was swimming.

She entered Anchors Aweigh to find a small sitting area to the left with the dining area across the way. Tonight, the dining was set up as one long table. She looked around to see if she recognized anyone, not that she thought she would, and was surprised to see one of the Marshalls in the middle of a small group. He was dressed very casually, with Bermuda shorts and a golf shirt. She never had caught his name which she thought was just as well since she shouldn't know him anyway.

Before she could cross over the room to introduce herself, the chef came out ringing a small silver bell announcing it was time for dinner.

The dinner was a blur of courses, each heavily laden with rum so that by the time dessert was served, Eva was quite drunk. She, of course, extended her congratulations and appreciation to the chef, assuring her everything was wonderful and bound to be a hit back in Nassau. Now, if only she could remember what she had!

Once she escaped the dinner and went out the door, the cool evening proved to be an elixir and helped her regain her bearings. She was painfully aware now was the time Slayder may make a move. It certainly was what the Marshalls hoped for. She looked for Snowflake but did not see him or his cronies. In fact, the main street was eerily vacant with only round pools of light thrown off by the intermittent street light illuminating her way home. She felt very alone. And then she saw him. A friendly face.

It was Bowers, who had just stepped out from the Compleat Angler allegedly for a cigarette. At least that was his cover as he watched her and casually scanned the street in front.

"Evening Eva. Care for a nightcap?"

She knew better, knew she had to get back to the Mahalo. Knew Calhoun, Hank and Bones would be getting worried. She knew, but yet…

"Sure"

What was she thinking? She knew better, knew it even as Bowers offered his arm to help steady her as they walked down the dock, knew it as he opened the door to the bar area where so many years ago, she had fled and later found love. Knew it even as she rounded the corner and there sat Slayder with no one else even in the bar. Knew it as she heard Bowers lock the door behind her. Knew it as a solitary tear fell.

Epilogue

My father, Calhoun, passed away in October 1976 after an eighteen month battle with colon cancer.

Captain Hank Nordlinger went on to captain several other boats before his retirement in 2005. He died in December 2017.

I last saw Eva in a Charleston, SC restaurant over 15 years ago with her two adult children. She was just as beautiful in middle age as she was in her 20's. She was a trophy even before that term existed.

I lost contact with Bones once the Mahalo sold.

Somewhere, this foursome continues their improbable adventures.

Tight Lines and Good Fishing

Boyd Hipp
August 2020

Acknowledgements

This story relies heavily upon the memories of many folks not the least of which was Captain Hank himself. It was a collaborative effort and as such much appreciation is due to Shirly Nordlinger, Larry Nordlinger, Lisa Nordlinger Jenkins, Mary Ladson Hipp Haddow, Gage Hipp Caulder, Teddy Hipp, Mary Jane Jacques, Mary Ann Bunton, Beth Hipp Clifton, Det Bowers and Neel Hipp with a special support nod to Kim Mann for her insights. Any criticism should lie solely with the author. Any resemblance to persons living or dead may or not be coincidental. You decide.

Appendix A

A good captain has to be a jack of many trades not the least of which is chef. Therefore, I would be remiss if I did not share: CAPTAIN HANK'S WORLD FAMOUS BBQ SHRIMP RECIPE (he said it was, therefore it was!)

4 Pounds large shrimp
Two Sticks Butter
¾ teaspoon red pepper (cayenne)
2 teaspoons garlic salt
2 teaspoons dry barbecue spice (Astor)
3 Teaspoons Worcestershire sauce
2 teaspoons paprika
1 teaspoon Lowery's seasoned pepper
1 teaspoon old Hickory smoked salt
1 chopped onion
1 lime squeezed
A splash of hot and spicy barbecue sauce (optional)
8 ounces chili sauce
1 teaspoon Tabasco Sauce
Place shrimp in shallow baking dish. Squeeze lime all over. Melt butter, add spices and mix. Pour over shrimp. Bake 20-24 minutes at 400 degrees. Baste often and serve with French Bread.
Make a stout Bacardi Rum and Coke with squeezed lime, hoist your glass and toast The Mahalo!

TO THE MAHALO!